Cursed with a poor sense of direction and a propensity to read, **Annie Claydon** spent much of her childhood lost in books. A degree in English Literature followed by a career in computing didn't lead directly to her perfect job—writing romance for Mills & Boon—but she has no regrets in taking the scenic route. She lives in London: a city where getting lost can be a joy.

Also by Annie Claydon

Saving Baby Amy
Forbidden Night with the Duke
Healed by the Single Dad Doc
From Doctor to Princess?
Firefighter's Christmas Baby
Resisting Her English Doc

London Heroes miniseries

Falling for Her Italian Billionaire
Second Chance with the Single Mum

Discover more at millsandboon.co.uk.

SECOND CHANCE WITH THE SINGLE MUM

ANNIE CLAYDON

MILLS & BOON

First published in Great Britain 2019
by Mills & Boon, an imprint of HarperCollins*Publishers*
1 London Bridge Street, London, SE1 9GF

Large Print edition 2019

© 2019 Annie Claydon

ISBN: 978-0-263-07863-3

MIX
Paper from
responsible sources
FSC™ C007454

This book is produced from independently certified
FSC™ paper to ensure responsible forest management. For
more information visit www.harpercollins.co.uk/green.

Printed and bound in Great Britain
by CPI Group (UK) Ltd, Croydon, CR0 4YY

To Joan, with love.

CHAPTER ONE

THE BENCH WAS shaded by trees, making it a pleasant place to sit on this hot summer's day. Raina Eliott was feeling anything but comfortable.

She could see the doorway of The Watchlight Trust's headquarters from her vantage point in the small leafy square, surrounded by three-storey Georgian houses, most of which had been converted to offices. She'd been watching it for the last hour, trying to pluck up the courage to go inside.

Asking a charity for help wasn't so difficult, was it? Nice people worked for charities. People who understood. But when one of those nice people who understood happened to be your ex-husband, everything became so much more complicated.

If she'd been asking for herself then it would have been simple. Raina would have hesitated at the door, and then walked away. But she'd promised to do her best for Anya, and at the moment, The Watchlight Trust wasn't just the best option, it was about the only option.

'Call yourself a mother?' She muttered the words to herself. Calling herself a mother was about the only good thing that had happened in the last few years, and was usually accompanied by a tingle of pleasure and the temptation to gather Anya up in her arms and hug her tight. And if she *did* call herself a mother then she had to do anything for her child, however difficult it was. She'd completed the charity's application form, and added all the supporting documents. Delivering them was just a matter of dropping them off at the reception desk.

She pulled the large manila envelope from her bag, staring at the address she'd written.

Alistair Duvall, Director
The Watchlight Trust

That was the stumbling block. Should she ask to speak to Alistair, to explain? And what exactly was there to explain? That she wouldn't have got back in touch with him after five years if it hadn't been for Anya? That she hoped he'd put their shared history out of his mind?

'Do it. Just deliver the envelope.' It wouldn't make any difference whether she spoke to Alistair or not, he'd know who she was as soon as he read the application. If he had a problem with working with his ex-wife then he'd just reject it.

Raina got to her feet, catching her breath as the door of The Watchlight Trust's offices opened. Two women appeared, stopping on the steps to talk to the man behind them. Alistair.

Still as handsome. Dark blond hair, cut a little shorter now and it suited him. He was smiling, and Raina imagined that the quiet warmth in his golden eyes was still there. His shirt was open at the neck, the sleeves rolled up, and just the sight of him made her feel as if her heart had stopped.

Alistair had followed the women down the steps, still talking, and they'd parted on the pavement. He looked at his watch and then made his way in the opposite direction. Maybe her heart *had* stopped, because Raina stumbled, zombie-like and unthinking, across the road towards him.

'Alistair...' His name caught in her throat and he kept walking. One more try...

She caught up with him, brushing his arm with her fingers. Alistair turned and she saw shock contort his face.

'Raina?' The idea that he would feel nothing at seeing her again was now impossible. He was staring at her, as if he'd just seen a ghost.

Raina swallowed hard. 'Alistair... I'm on my way to deliver something to you...'

Raina didn't blame him for looking at the envelope with mistrust. The last envelope she'd sent him had been their divorce papers. There was nothing for it but to grasp the nettle, however much it stung.

'I... It's an application form. I have a daughter, Anya, and I want to apply to have her included on the prosthetics project that you're running with The Watchlight Trust. If you can forgive me enough to look at it, that is...' Suddenly it seemed more than she had any right to ask.

'I should be the one asking for your forgiveness.' He was looking at her thoughtfully.

'I don't think that's true.' She shivered in the heat of the sun. Alistair might not want to talk about it, but neither of them could deny that she was the one who'd walked out on him.

Suddenly he came to his senses. This was the Alistair she knew, a man who could make the right decision in a moment, and would always use his humanity in doing so.

'If your daughter needs us, then we're here for her, Raina. Nothing else matters.'

'Thank you. Anya's three years old, she'll be four soon and…' Raina saw a pulse begin to beat at the side of Alistair's eye. The maths wasn't difficult, and Anya had been conceived just months after their divorce.

Raina took a breath. She needed to start at the beginning, however much that beginning hurt. 'She's Andrew and Theresa's child. They were killed in the same road accident where Anya lost her left hand and part of her forearm. I've adopted her.'

Alistair's eyes flared with shock and then softened again. 'I'm so sorry, Raina. I liked your brother and his wife very much, they were good people.'

'I…should have let you know…about the accident. I'm sorry…'

'You had more than enough to deal with. Don't give it another thought.'

Raina was trembling so much that all she

could do was to hold out the envelope, hoping that Alistair would take it. He looked at his watch again, as if maybe that would tell him something, and gave her a tight smile.

'Look, I've just got out of a long meeting, and I was about to pick up a sandwich. Why don't you walk with me? I'd like to hear a bit more about Anya and what you feel she needs from us. Then give me that.' He gestured towards the envelope.

'Yes. Thank you, Alistair.' Raina stuffed the envelope back into her bag, and he began to walk towards the coffee shop at the far corner of the square.

Alistair must need to gather his thoughts as well. She had presented him with one shock after another, and it was hardly fair. He was silent, clearly dealing with it all in the way that Alistair always dealt with things. Quiet, measured and uncommunicative.

He held the door of the coffee shop open for her, and the coolness of the air-conditioning made her shiver. Sitting on a park bench and drinking takeaway coffee for an hour was catching up on her, and Raina excused herself, making a welcome dash for the ladies' room.

'That's the worst of it over...' She whispered the words as confidently as she could, trying to persuade her own reflection in the mirror over the basin. But the reflection was having none of it and Raina couldn't help but agree. Something told her that she hadn't even scratched the surface yet.

The divorce had been bitter. Raina's pregnancy had been unexpected, and her own joy had blinded her to Alistair's concerns about whether they were ready, and how they would manage financially. Then sudden pain had turned into the nightmare of discovering that the pregnancy was ectopic and the baby couldn't be saved. Alistair had retreated into himself, showing only concern for Raina and hardly mentioning their lost child. The suspicion that he might think, deep down, that this was all for the best had poisoned everything, and as she'd recovered her strength, Raina had raged at him, venting her own pain.

It was only after she'd left him that Raina had found out about the infection. It had meant that one of her fallopian tubes had had to be removed, and since the other was partially blocked, she'd be unlikely to ever conceive again. And now she had to go out there and persuade Alistair that she could work with him, and he should give Anya the chance she so badly needed. Raina splashed cool water onto her cheeks, dabbing them dry with a tissue from her bag.

She'd thought that Alistair might spend the time choosing a sandwich, but instead he was holding two cups of takeaway coffee. Putting one into her hand, he gestured towards the door.

'Would you mind if we walked? I've been shut up inside all morning...'

'Walking would be nice.' At least it would give her something to do with her feet. And the coffee would give her something to do with her hands. All she needed to worry about now was her tongue. She took a sip of the coffee. Plenty of frothed milk and a little sugar. It should be no surprise that Alistair remembered the way she liked it, but still it was a shock, reminding Raina of the scale of the task she'd taken on. Being with Alistair would be an exercise in remembering all the things she'd tried so hard to forget.

* * *

Alistair had almost jumped out of his skin when he'd seen Raina. How many times had he thought he'd glimpsed her in a crowd, and then looked again to find it wasn't her? But this was no ghost.

Alistair guessed that if she'd had any options that didn't involve him, she would have taken them. He should remember that. Despite her obvious agitation, she looked well. When he'd last seen her she'd had rings of fatigue under her eyes, and she couldn't meet his gaze. But now she was more the way he'd first seen her, a dark-haired, dark-eyed beauty who'd taken his breath away. Divorce clearly suited her.

It was a bitter thought. It knocked him off balance even more than the music in the coffee shop, which rendered him almost completely deaf and had changed his mind about sitting down to talk. He needed to be able to hear everything that Raina was saying.

The pavement was only a little better, but if they avoided the main roads, the traffic noise wouldn't be too distracting. If he stayed on her left side, then his 'good' ear could catch most of what she said.

'You've read about the project on our website?' Of course she had. Raina was nothing if not thorough.

She nodded a yes, maybe voicing it too, and Alistair slowed his pace to a stroll. Watching the words form on her lips would help fill in the gaps in his hearing.

'Then you'll know that this project marks the start of a new and important expansion in the activities of The Watchlight Trust. Up till now, our primary focus has been on helping people in the accident and rescue services, but we've always known that many of the techniques we use have a much wider application. My co-director, Gabriel DeMarco, and I have been working towards realising that potential for some time now.'

He was practically quoting from the website, and she'd read that already. But in a world that had suddenly turned upside down he might be forgiven for finding a few solid facts reassuring.

'Our development team is currently housed in our offices, and we have medical services based at our own clinic next door. Our long-term aim is to create a separate division of the charity, whose remit is to explore innovative technologies and make them available to patients.'

'It's a bold step. And one that will benefit a lot of people.'

Alistair had thought so too. And then sudden hearing loss had turned his working day into a miasma of half-heard sentences, a constant struggle to keep up. Gabriel had done his best to help, but it had only made Alistair feel even more useless, relegated to standing by and watching while others made the bold steps that it took to realise the project that meant so much to him.

But now he had a purpose. Raina was unaware of the nature of the challenge she'd thrown at him, but that didn't mean he couldn't rise to it and find a way to help her.

'We're still refining our product and procedures, and we're hoping to be able to learn with the parents and children we select for the pilot project.'

'I'd welcome the chance to learn, and to contribute as much as I'm able as well.'

Staring at her lips had its disadvantages. He could make out what she was saying better, but it reminded Alistair of all the other times he'd studied her face. Locked in each other's arms, immersed in each other...

Enough! There was no going back, and the present was more than enough to deal with. Alistair forced his thoughts back to the child. She was what mattered.

'Has your daughter been fitted with a prosthetic yet?'

'Yes, six months ago. It took some time for it to be made, and the first one she was given didn't fit properly, so we had to wait again for it to be adjusted. By the time we did get it right, Anya was determined she didn't want it, however much we tried to encourage her. 3D printing is a much faster and more flexible process and I think it may be more appropriate for Anya's needs.'

'So tell me why you think she should have one.' Alistair stopped walking, facing her so that he could concentrate on Raina's answer. It was the question he'd asked every parent and he'd received a variety of replies.

Raina smiled, suddenly sure of herself. 'I don't think she *should* do anything. I want her to have a choice about if and when she uses a prosthetic, and she won't have that choice unless she learns what she can do with one. She's starting to reach out into the world, and I want her to know about the different options she has.'

Raina pressed her lips together, tilting her jaw slightly. The look was so familiar to him that Alistair had to swallow a smile. Raina had made up her mind, and she was challenging him to disagree, but what she wanted for her daughter was exactly in line with his own thinking.

'That's our approach too. We believe that the speed and low cost of 3D pr0.inting can help us address some of the issues involved with children who have previously rejected prosthetics, but we're not limiting our expectations to any one outcome.'

'Neither am I. I just want…' A car roared past, drowning out the rest of the sentence.

'Sorry, I didn't hear you.'

'I want Anya to be happy and fulfilled. That's the only expectation I'm not giving up on.'

He should have known that, without having to ask. Raina was a good doctor, and she never gave up on anyone. How could she be expected to give up on her own daughter?

Alistair started to walk again, and their route took them onto the main road, which ran along the bank of the Thames. He motioned Raina towards the crossing, noticing that her lips were moving and wondering if she was saying anything of any importance. He decided not to ask. He'd save the *I didn't hear* for when he knew it was needed.

The wide pavement on the other side of the road was bordered by the river, and Alistair looked for a quiet place that they might sit. His head was buzzing, and he'd made his way towards a bench, standing in the shadow of Cleopatra's Needle, before he realised where they were.

'I have half an hour. Can you meet me on the bench by the river?'

One or the other of them had brought coffee then, too. They had been young doctors working long shifts and they'd needed the caffeine and the fresh air almost as much as they'd needed the love that had been in each other's eyes.

It was too late to move now. Raina had sat down next to him, sipping the last dregs of her coffee. He shifted around on the bench so that he was facing her.

'We're hoping to involve parents very closely in this project. Would that be a problem for you time-wise?'

Raina shook her head. 'I've taken a few years off work to care for Anya. She's my only priority, and I can spend as much time as it takes to make this a success.'

She'd had such a promising career, and Raina had put that all on hold. It didn't much surprise Alistair, but he felt shamed by it. He wondered whether he would have thought twice about doing the same.

'Can you tell me a little about your daughter?'

'Well, as I said, Anya's three years old. And she's beautiful…' Raina smiled suddenly. 'She's becoming so curious about the world. Look…'

She took her phone from her pocket, flipping through photos. Alistair was about to tell her that he didn't need to see photographs when Raina held out the phone.

A little girl, with dark curls and brown eyes, smiling gleefully as she inspected sea shells on a beach. She was so like Raina that it almost hurt to look, but in that moment he knew that if things had been different, and this had been his and Raina's child, he would have given up everything for the little girl as well.

The temptation to tell her right now that she and her daughter had a place on the pilot scheme almost overwhelmed him. But there was a process, and all applications had to go through the assessment procedures.

'And you've completed your application?'

'Yes, and all the supporting documents are there too. I've spoken with Anya's consultant about it, and he thinks that it's a way forward for her. The kind of prosthetics you're producing aren't widely available yet and when I showed him your website he agreed that The Watchlight Trust's patient-led approach made your scheme a very good option for Anya.'

She pulled the large manila envelope with his name on it out of her bag, opening it and taking out a folder and handing it to him. The application was neatly bound together with typed pages, which no doubt gave all the details about her daughter's injury and her medical needs. But the front page gave little doubt about what

Raina thought was most important. This photograph showed the little girl with crayons and a drawing pad. Raina's whole focus was on what she *could* do, and her potential to do more.

Suddenly he realised that Raina had been speaking…

'Sorry…what was that?' It was tempting to just smile and nod when he didn't hear something, and ninety per cent of the time that worked well. But the other ten per cent of the time it wasn't what people were looking for in an answer.

'I just said…that I want to thank you. For talking to me about Anya.'

'You're welcome.' He went back to flipping through the papers. He'd learned that most people responded well when he told them about his deafness, but something stopped him this time. Maybe Raina's attitude, so positive despite all she'd been through. His own problems didn't matter.

He went to look up at her and jumped suddenly as he heard the sound of rushing water coming from the road behind him. Before he knew what he was doing he stretched out his hand to shield Raina.

Then he realised that the sound was coming from the river. Staring at it, trying to marry the sound with what he saw, he jumped again as he felt Raina touch his arm lightly.

'Are you okay?'

'Yeah… I should be getting back to the office, though.' He didn't have that much to do there, and a small voice at the back of his head was telling him that this wasn't the first time he'd retreated into his work to avoid a difficult conversation with Raina. Alistair dismissed it, taking one last swig from his coffee cup.

'As I'm heading up the project, there's a clear conflict of interest here, and I want to make sure that everything's entirely above board. So I'm going to give your application to my co-director Gabriel DeMarco for assessment. He'll be getting back to you within a week.'

'Thank you, Alistair. You've been very kind.'

He wanted to tell Raina that he once would have done anything for her, and in the last half-hour he'd realised that nothing had changed. But that was beyond inappropriate. He trusted Gabriel to do the right thing, and that he'd handle Raina's application fairly. He had to step back now.

CHAPTER TWO

ALISTAIR HAD GIVEN her a better reception than she deserved. But he seemed so remote, hardly hearing what she said at times.

What had Raina expected? That the divorce and all that had led up to it would just melt away? A person could forget a lot in five years. Not that much, though.

'What's going on? Over there…?' He didn't react to her question but when Raina pointed towards a group of people that was forming by the stone parapet at the side of the pavement, he turned to look.

'We should go and see. Perhaps someone's hurt.' Raina got to her feet, looping her bag over her shoulder.

When they'd first been married, it would have taken just an exchange of glances. Young doctors who wanted to save the world, and who would rush towards any potential emergency, believing that together they were indestructible. It wasn't like Alistair to hesitate.

Raina wasn't going to wait for him to sum the situation up, though. She ran over to the knot of people that had formed.

'I'm a doctor. Is anyone hurt?' No one turned and the wall of backs prevented her from seeing what had happened. Then she felt an arm around her shoulder. Alistair the rock. Pushing through the crowd and taking her with him.

'What's the matter?' A woman was holding a child of about two years old, gesturing frantically towards the deep granite parapet between the pavement and the river. She took no notice of Alistair's question, but a man replied.

'A kid's climbed over the barrier…'

Quite how he'd managed to do that wasn't clear, but when Raina leaned over she could see a boy of around six clinging to the other side. He began to slip, his feet scrabbling for a hold, and the woman screamed.

'Hold on, sweetheart… Please…someone help him.'

Raina felt, rather than saw, Alistair thrust the envelope with her grant application back into her hands. Climbing across the deep coping stones on the top of the parapet, he slid carefully down the other side, making his way across to the boy.

'Give me a leg up, will you?' Raina turned to the man standing next to her and suddenly Alistair seemed to remember that she existed, and looked up.

'Stay there, Raina. Anya needs you home tonight.'

There had been a time when they wouldn't have thought twice about it. She would have been right there next to him. Now it seemed that Alistair acted alone.

But he was right, Anya *did* need her to come home tonight. How many times had Raina hesitated and looked again before crossing the road, knowing that Anya couldn't lose another parent. And the ledge that Alistair was now edging along towards the boy was too narrow for a second person to be of any use.

He almost lost his footing, stopping to regain his hold. Suddenly Alistair looked up again, his golden-brown eyes searching for her.

'Easy does it. You're nearly there.'

He nodded, carefully moving closer to the boy. Just as it seemed that Alistair could reach out and touch him, his mother called out to him. The boy looked up, lost his balance and toppled backwards, twisting as he fell and landing flat on his stomach in the river.

Alistair didn't hesitate. Kicking off his shoes, he jumped, disappearing underwater for a few heart-stopping seconds. Then he surfaced, looking around for the boy.

He didn't have much time. The boy had landed amongst some floating debris and the swell of the tide had washed him against a large piece of wood. He struggled weakly in the water, seeming stunned by the impact, and then was still, floating face down. He was already starting to drown and soon he'd begin to sink. If that happened it would be a miracle if Alistair found him in the murky water. Raina screamed Alistair's name, pointing to the boy.

He looked up, and then in the direction in which she was pointing. A few strong strokes, and Alistair had the boy, lifting him up in his arms so that his head was clear of the water. The child started to choke and fight, but Alistair held onto him.

'He's choking… He's going to drown…' The

boy's mother was behind her, clinging to her other child, her eyes fixed on her son.

'My colleague's a strong swimmer and he's a doctor.' Raina tried to calm the woman down. 'And if he's choking that means he's breathing.' The instinctive drowning response was a silent struggle, one that often didn't alarm onlookers.

Raina looked around, trying to see how Alistair could get out of the water. The wash from boats travelling up and down the river was swelling against him, and he and the boy were in danger of being thrown against the river wall.

'Hey!' A pleasure boat was moored at a jetty nearby and she shouted at the top of her voice to the people on board. 'Hey, there's someone in the water...'

There was a scuffle of confusion on board the boat, and then a man ran to the railing, carrying a lifebelt. Throwing it into the water with as much force as he could, it landed with a splash, and Alistair started to swim towards it.

Raina ran for the jetty, clambering down the angled wooden ramp that led down to the craft. A man blocked her path.

'I'm a doctor. Let me through.' The man nodded, taking her arm and guiding her to where the boy was being lifted up onto the deck and laid down on a folded fire blanket. Alistair was still in the water and she barely had time to glance in his direction before the child claimed her attention.

A policeman had arrived on the scene and was shepherding the boy's mother towards them. The boy started to cry when he saw her, reaching for her. 'It's all right, Jamie. Let the doctor take a look at you.' The woman took hold of his hand.

He'd had a shock, and he'd obviously swallowed some water, which wasn't good. But he was breathing and seemed alert, despite the bump on the back of his head. Raina examined him as well as she could, and then sat back on her heels, looking up at the policeman.

'He seems okay, but he'll need to be checked over at the hospital.' The policeman nodded, taking his radio from its clip and speaking into it.

'Will he be all right?' Jamie's mother caught hold of her sleeve, an imploring look in her eyes. Raina had seen that look so many times before, but hadn't really understood the agony behind it until she'd become a mother to Anya.

'He's breathing, and he's safe.' Raina started with the good news. 'But I want that bump on his head looked at. The doctors will be checking to see if there's any water in his lungs, and they'll have to clean any cuts very carefully to avoid infection.'

'Thank you, Doctor.' Jamie's mother held his hand while Raina wrapped blankets around him that the pleasure boat's crew had brought. She could hear the sound of a siren, and it seemed that they were in luck and the ambulance would be here soon.

As soon as she'd handed over to the ambulance crew, Raina looked for Alistair. She found him, sitting further along the deck, his arms resting on his knees and his head bowed. Someone had brought him a blanket and it lay draped across his shoulders. As Raina reached to pull it around him, he looked up.

There had been a time when she'd lived for the smile that flickered across his face and the golden heat of his eyes. Right now that time seemed much closer than she'd thought it would ever be again.

'Hi, there. Are you all right?'

'I'm okay. How's the boy?'

Raina glanced across, and saw Jamie cling-ing to his mother, responding to the ambulance crew's questions. 'He doesn't seem too much the worse for wear. But he needs to be seen at the hospital.'

Alistair nodded. He knew that Jamie was at risk from all kinds of infections from the dirty water, and that dry drowning could occur hours after a child was pulled from the water and seemed fully recovered from the experi-ence. Not to mention the possibility of a con-cussion.

'The ambulance crew are dealing with it?' He was cupping his hand over his ear as if checking exactly how much he could hear.

'Yes, they've got everything under control. They know exactly what the situation is and what the doctors need to look for. Is there something wrong with your ears?'

He shook his head. Something *was* wrong and it was more than just being wet through and covered in grime from the river. Raina wanted to reach out and hug him for his brav-ery, and then find out what the matter was and make it right. Instead, she pulled a paper handkerchief from her bag, dabbing at a small cut beside his left eye.

'Don't, Raina.' His tone wasn't unkind but he shied away from her impatiently. 'It's all right…'

'So Jamie's at risk of infection from the dirty water but you're not. What are you, Dr Invincible?'

Raina bit her lip. That joke belonged to a time when they had been married. It didn't sound half as apt now they were divorced. But seeing him like this… It awakened every protective instinct she had and it was killing her that Alistair wouldn't take any help from her.

It was Alistair all over, though. When things had got tough when she'd become pregnant and then lost the baby, he'd shut down. When all Raina had wanted him to do was to share his feelings, when she'd wanted him to feel the same wild grief as she had, he'd pushed her away.

She swallowed hard. That had been then, and this was now. She was a doctor, and she had someone who might be hurt sitting right in front of her. That justified her professional concern.

Suddenly she could think clearly again. Put all the little pieces of the puzzle together to make a place to start. She turned her head away from him, speaking clearly.

'You can't hear, can you?'

'What was that?' Alistair frowned impatiently.

'I said…' She faced him squarely. 'You can't hear. Can you, Alistair?'

So much for thinking that he'd been doing a pretty good job in covering up. If he hadn't been wet through and shivering from the shock of seeing young Jamie plunge into the water when he'd just been a hair's breadth away from reaching him, Alistair might have been able to brush the question off. But right now he wanted someone to know.

Not just *someone*. He could have told the man who'd helped him out of the water and gone to fetch the blanket, but he'd had no inclination to do so. He wanted Raina to know. He wanted that sweet, dark-eyed concern that made his heart lurch.

'It's…it's not a result of being in the water. It's a pre-existing condition.' Maybe if he kept this professional, he could ignore the tingle in his fingertips. The urge to have Raina kiss away all of his aches and pains, and all of the fears for a future that was anything but silent but which contained too much white noise to make any sense of what he did hear.

She gave him a searching look. 'And I'd be right in saying you've seen someone about this?'

'Yes, you would.' However much he wanted her to stop caring, he felt it warm him. 'I went to get it checked out as soon as it happened.'

He could almost see the cogs turning in Raina's brain. As they did so, a look of determination crept across her face. 'It's none of my business…'

Then he'd make it her business. The urge to tell her was fast overcoming the feeling that he didn't want to betray what seemed to him to be a weakness.

'It's SSHL.'

'When did this happen?'

'Almost exactly two months ago. I felt a bit of pressure in my ear and thought I might have a cold. Then I heard a pop, and realised I was completely deaf in my left ear. My hearing's impaired in my right ear but it's not as bad. I've had all the tests and there's nothing else wrong...' Just that he was deaf. *That* was wrong with him, although no one could see it.

'So you're a textbook case for sudden sensorineural hearing loss.'

Alistair nodded. 'It improved a little during the first month, but I'm reckoning that what I have now is...pretty much what I'll always have going forward. I'll be getting a hearing aid soon, and that might help a bit with directionality.'

Raina nodded. 'You have tinnitus?'

'Yeah. That seems to be improving.' Alistair wasn't sure whether it was or not. It was probably just wishful thinking, born of the loss he felt over the thought that he might never be able to appreciate silence again, because of the high-pitched ringing in his ears. That, combined with the faraway bubbling sound and the occasional ticking that seemed to come from about two inches behind his right ear, turned silence into an almost unbearable clamour.

'Your ability to focus on other things will improve when you get your hearing aid.' Raina's tone was matter-of-fact, but the look in her eyes...

It was the look that could make him forget about everything else and believe that there was nothing else in the world but her. No sound but the sound of her voice. No feeling that didn't emanate from her touch...

'Yeah. That's what my audiologist says. I'm not getting my hopes up too much.'

She nodded, thoughtfully. 'We should have gone somewhere quieter to talk.'

'I heard what I needed to hear. And I have to get used to functioning in any situation.'

'So you're throwing yourself in at the deep end?'

Alistair was about to protest that he was doing nothing of the sort, and that he could hear her perfectly well now. But that was because Raina was doing exactly what he usually had to ask people to do—facing him and speaking clearly. She'd always given him what he'd needed...

And he hadn't given her what she'd needed. He'd let her go because someone else could give her the family that she'd so wanted and that he just hadn't been ready for. But now, even if he was struggling to find his place in a world that suddenly seemed strange and remote, he could give her something.

'I want you to go back to the office. Ask to see Heidi Walker, she's Gabriel's and my assistant. Give her your application and ask her to pass it to Gabriel to read this evening. I'll give him a call later.'

'That can wait until tomorrow, Alistair. I need to get you home first.'

He was already beginning to shiver in the afternoon sun, and despite himself Alistair wanted Raina to make a fuss of him. But he'd already revealed more than he wanted her to know, and he just wanted her to go now, before he was tempted to let anything else slip.

'Pass me the envelope. And do you have a pen?'

Raina shot him a look that made it very clear that her compliance didn't mean she agreed, and plunged her hand into her bag, producing a plastic ballpoint. She balanced her application on the top of her bag to provide a makeshift writing surface and Alistair scribbled a note to Heidi, trying not to get any drips onto the envelope.

She was staring at him dumbly, clearly about to argue with him. But there was no point in listening to Raina tell him that she wouldn't leave while he was wet through, bleeding and confused by the sounds around him. They were the exact reasons he wanted her to go.

'The police officer came over while you were with Jamie, and he's radioed for a car to take me home.'

'But...' Raina wasn't giving up that easily. She had to, though, because if The Watchlight Trust was going to be able to help her daughter, then their relationship had to be completely professional. All about the little girl's needs and not his.

'Go, Raina.' He spoke quickly, before he had a chance to change his mind. 'I want you to go.'

There had been moments when Alistair's mask of self-reliance had slipped. When the thought that he wanted her there, with him, had thundered through Raina's head. But now he was cool, and more than a little commanding.

He could protest that he was all right as much as he wanted. It was basic medical necessity to clean a cut that had been submersed in dirty water, and he could like it or not. If he didn't like it he could jump straight back into the river.

Raina got to her feet, stuffing the envelope back into her bag, and walked over to the ambulance paramedics, who were getting ready to go. After making sure that Jamie didn't need her, she asked for some antiseptic wipes, and was given a small pack of them, along with a pair of disposable gloves.

Returning to Alistair, she tore the wrapper open. He seemed about to argue and then obviously thought better of it. At least he still knew when to keep his mouth shut.

He winced as she cleaned the cut on his face, but said nothing, and when she told him to show her his hands, he held them out silently, turning them so she could check them thoroughly.

'Did you swallow any water?'

'No. It's just as filthy as it looks and I decided not to stop for a drink.'

'Take these.' Raina put the rest of the antiseptic wipes down next to him on the deck. 'Clean that cut again when you get home, and make sure to do to the same with any other abrasions.'

'Yes. Thanks. You should go. The office will be closing soon.'

'Shall I tell them what's happened? So they won't be expecting you back?'

'Yes, thanks. Say I'll be back first thing to-morrow.'

There was no point in telling him that he might want to spend tomorrow morning easing out any aches and pains and making sure that his dive into the water hadn't resulted in any other ill-effects. Alistair had made it clear that it wasn't her place any more and he was right.

'Is your phone working?'

Alistair reached into his pocket, and took out his phone. The screen was cracked, and water dripped from it onto the deck.

'Doesn't look like it. But I've a backup at home, in case I lose this one.'

That was Alistair all over. He was all about the work, and nothing got in the way of that. A broken phone was a trifling obstacle when compared to a broken marriage, and he'd managed to spend enough of his energies on work then. Raina swallowed down her resentment and reached into her bag.

'I'd like you to let me know that you're okay.' She scribbled her mobile number onto a scrap of paper and tucked it into the packet of antiseptic wipes.

'I'll text you as soon as I've got home and taken a shower.'

His tone indicated that there was nothing more to say. She had to go now, and show him that she could follow his instructions, because that was what Raina was going to have to do if Anya was accepted onto The Watchlight Trust's project.

'Thanks. Take care, Alistair.' Raina got to her feet, trying not to look at him in case that made her want to stay. Standing aside to let the ambulance crew take Jamie and his mother up the gangway to their vehicle, she didn't look back until she'd reached the pavement.

Then she couldn't help herself. Her knees were grimy from kneeling on the wet deck and she pushed her skirt up to rub at them with a tissue, as an excuse to stop and turn. As she did so, she saw a police car draw up, and an officer get out and make her way down onto the boat.

That was Alistair's lift home. She saw him get to his feet, and a couple of the pleasure boat's crew came to shake his hand. Then the policewoman ushered him towards the gangway, smiling at him as she did so. That was Raina's invitation to leave, before Alistair saw that she was still there.

CHAPTER THREE

THERE HAD BEEN a time when Raina's touch would have made everything all right. Instead, Alistair opted for standing under the shower for half an hour, trying to wash off the smell of the river.

An impenetrable barrier stood between them now. Raina had brought him such happiness, and when she'd left he'd felt nothing but pain and grief. Turning to his work as a way out had only reinforced his belief that he could never be the husband and father he wanted to be.

Alistair scrubbed his body with a towel and put on clean clothes. Somehow a trace of the river still remained, but if he ignored it then it would probably go away. His eyes still stung a little, and he blinked as he picked up the slip of paper that Raina had left.

Raina Elliot… He noticed that she was using her maiden name now. That wasn't much of a surprise, particularly since her niece's surname was Elliot too. If nothing else it sent a message for the little girl who was now her daughter.

'Raina Duvall. You like it…?'

He'd whispered the words in her ear as they'd danced together on their wedding night, and she'd smiled up at him.

'I love it. What else do you think I married you for?'

He'd known then that there had been many other things. *Love* had just about covered it. True love. Devoted love. Making love…

And when he'd given his name to her, he'd suddenly begun to like it a lot more. Up until then it had just been something he'd inherited from his father, along with a chunk of DNA and a propensity to spend all his energies at work.

But Raina had taken the name and made it hers. She had been a creature of warm summer days who'd left the taste of cool raindrops on his lips. Her ability to occasionally thunder and roar had all been a part of her free spirit, and when the storm had passed, everything would be washed clean. Raina had shown her feelings in a way that he'd never been able to, and that was what had broken them apart.

That, and Alistair's failure. He hadn't known his father all that well, but his mother had always told him that he was a lot like him. Being like his father meant he'd be a good provider, Alistair had grown up in a comfortable, affluent home. It also meant that his family would always take second place to his work. Alistair could barely recall one childhood memory that included his father.

When Raina had unexpectedly become pregnant, Alistair had tried to tell himself that he just wasn't ready, as if somehow the passage of time might change his nature. The truth of it was that he was more like his father than he wanted to admit, driven and wrapped up with his work. He'd been busy at work, his phone switched off, on the day that Raina had lost their baby. If there was one thing in his life that Alistair could go back and change, it would be that. Raina had gone through all that agony alone.

The thing he wouldn't change was letting her go. There was someone out there who could be a father for the children Raina wanted so badly, and it was only right that Alistair should step aside, however much it hurt.

He picked up his phone, tapping her number into the contacts list. He'd always thought that Raina would become a mother in less tragic circumstances. But the love he'd seen on her face when she'd shown him the photographs of her little girl told Alistair that she wouldn't be bound by regrets.

That probably included him as well. And wanting to hear her voice, wanting to feel her cool fingers washing him clean, wasn't the way to go. She'd asked him to text and that was what he'd do. He typed in a message telling her that he was home, and his phone pinged almost immediately.

You okay?

No, not really. The aches and pains in his body were nothing. The ache in his heart wouldn't go away.

Yes. Fine, thanks.

That was the end of it. Alistair sent the text and then realised that he had a question of his own.

You delivered the application?

Yes. Heidi said she'd give it straight to Gabriel.

Good. Gabriel would probably have read it by now, and Alistair should give him a call.

Thanks. We'll be in touch.

Thank you. Again.

That didn't really require an answer. Alistair closed the text screen and dialled Gabriel's number.

At the other end of the line, Raina was frowning. It was all very well to keep this on a businesslike footing, but Alistair seemed to be going out of his way to deflect any enquiries about his well-being.

'Mummy…' Anya was sitting in the bath, and she reached up, brushing Raina's face with her hand. Her instinctive grasp of how Raina was feeling surpassed her ability to understand those feelings.

'It's just a text, sweetie.'

'Who texted, Mummy?'

Raina made a face at Anya, and she giggled, splashing her bath water all over Raina's shirt.

'It was someone I went to see today while you were at Grandma's house. His name is Alistair.'

'Is he naughty?'

'Yes. Very… But we're not going to worry about that. Let's get you out of the bath now and into your pyjamas.'

'Naughty Alistair,' Anya chirped, and Raina winced. She'd spoken without thinking. Perhaps if she didn't say the word *naughty* for the next week, then Anya would forget all about that. If they did get through the selection process, she didn't want Anya referring to Alistair as naughty while he was in earshot.

'No, sorry, sweetie, I got it wrong. It's really *nice* Alistair.'

'Did you send him kisses?'

'No, kisses are just for when we text Grandma.' Kisses would be asking for trouble. Asking for the kind of heartbreak that should only be experienced once in a lifetime, as a lesson on what to avoid the next time around.

'Then he must be naughty…' Anya gave her a cheeky grin and Raina's heart melted. Lifting Anya out of the bath, she wrapped her in a towel, hugging her tight. Kisses were off limits and so was any kind of naughtiness. The only person that mattered was Anya.

'Is that Raina?'

'Yes.' Raina had been grabbing at her phone every time it had rung for the last few days, and every time she did, it wasn't Alistair. This time was no exception.

'My name's Gabriel DeMarco. I work with Alistair at The Watchlight Trust, and he's passed your application for your daughter on to me. I understand that you're interested in taking part in our trials for the prosthetic limbs project.'

'Yes…yes, I am.' Raina held her breath, sitting back on her heels. Anya continued with the task of scooping soil into the plant pots that were laid out in front of them on the lawn, blithely unaware that her life might be about to change.

'We'd like to explore that possibility a little further. If you're still interested?'

'Yes!' She probably shouldn't shout at him on the phone. Anya looked up at her and echoed the word, squealing with laughter. 'Sorry…yes, I am still interested.'

Gabriel's deep chuckle sounded in her ear. 'You both sound as enthusiastic about the project as we are. There is one thing I'd like to discuss with you first, if you don't mind. It's a personal matter...'

Alistair. What had he said to Gabriel? Raina swallowed down her paranoia. She had no choice but to trust the man she'd once known so intimately. 'You mean my relationship with Alistair?'

'I do.' Gabriel sounded a little relieved that he hadn't had to explain. 'Alistair's taken a step back from the selection process, so as to avoid any possible conflict of interest. If Anya's selected for the project, then I'll be Anya's doctor of record, and I'll be responsible for prescribing the type of prosthetic that best suits her needs. But as Alistair's heading up the project, you would inevitably find yourself working closely with him.'

It was all becoming a reality. Raina hadn't dared think too much about the prospect of working with Alistair, but now she had to.

There was nothing for it but the truth. 'Alistair and I have had our differences... obviously. But I've always respected him, and this means far too much to me to allow any personal issues to get in the way. I'd consider it a privilege to work with him.'

That would have to do. Raina held her breath, wondering if it was enough, and heard Gabriel's deep chuckle at the other end of the line.

'Since that's pretty much what Alistair said, I think I can safely tick that question off my list. We've already interviewed a number of families for the project, and I'm wondering whether you'd be able to bring Anya in to see us tomorrow?'

'Yes, any time that suits you...' Raina felt her heart jolt up a notch. She and Anya had obviously made it through to the second stage of the process.

'Eleven o'clock? You'll be meeting with me and Maya Powell. Maya's a consultant in rehabilitation medicine, and she's collaborated with us before over the years. It's not her intention to have any ongoing involvement with families selected for the project, but she's donated some of her time to help with the screening and assessment process.'

In other words, Alistair wouldn't be there. That was one hurdle that Raina didn't have to negotiate just yet. 'Eleven would be fine, thank you.'

'Great, I'll see you then. Would you choose a favourite toy for Anya and bring that along too. We'd like to get to know her...'

Raina sat, staring at the phone after Gabriel had ended the call. This was all good. It seemed that Alistair had kept his promise and wasn't going to stand in their way.

'We did it, Anya. I think it must have been that cute smile of yours.'

Anya was unimpressed. 'Mummy, can we put the plants in the pots?'

Raina bent to kiss the little girl's cheek. 'Yes, we're going to do it right now. And tomorrow we're going on the train to see someone. *Nice* Gabriel.'

Gabriel was waiting for them in the reception area, a tall, dark-haired man whose natural expression seemed to be a smile. He ushered them through a bright, open-plan space to two glass-walled offices at the far end, making for the one that was shaded from view by blinds. As they entered, a woman rose from the informal seating area at one end.

'Raina, this is Maya Powell.'

Both Gabriel and Maya were relaxed and smiling, and drinks and pastries were laid out on the coffee table, around which a sofa and two leather easy chairs were arranged. But Raina wasn't fooled. This was serious business, and the child-friendly atmosphere was for Anya's benefit.

Maya shook Raina's hand and then bent down towards the little girl. 'You must be Anya. I'm Maya. We have a drink for you here, if you'd like one.'

Anya whispered a *hello*, clinging to Raina's hand and leaning against her legs. Raina resisted the impulse to push her forward, hoping she'd get over her shyness.

'Would you like to play with your bricks, sweetie?' She pulled the box of bricks from her bag, putting it on the coffee table, and Anya stared at it uncertainly.

'Bricks…?' When Raina turned, Gabriel's eyes were shining. Sitting down on the sofa, he ran his finger across the top of the box. 'Bricks are my favourite. Would you show me, Anya?'

His enthusiasm was so infectious Anya let go of Raina's hand, running across to the box of bricks and opening it. Gabriel grinned, craning over to see inside, and Raina breathed a sigh of relief as Anya began to empty the box, showing Gabriel the bricks.

'These are fantastic.' He addressed his comment to no one in particular and then smiled at Raina. 'I'll be a father soon.'

Maya chuckled, rolling her eyes. 'Is there anyone in London you *haven't* managed to tell yet, Gabriel?'

'No. Probably not.' Gabriel was busy sorting out the bricks. 'Where do you get these?'

'You go to the shop and buy them.' Anya's tone implied that this was the kind of information that anyone should know.

'Do you? Which shop?'

Anya shrugged and Raina supplied the answer. 'You'll find these in any toy shop. You won't be needing them for a while, though. Congratulations.' It was nice to see a man so happy at the prospect of becoming a father.

'Thank you. We went for the three-month scan yesterday, and my wife's given me the all-clear to share the news. It was a complete surprise.'

A lump settled in Raina's throat. Her pregnancy had been a complete surprise too, but it would have been difficult to imagine Alistair making enquiries about building bricks, and unable to stop himself from telling everyone he met.

She'd never forgotten her lost child, but right now she had to think about Anya. Maya waved her to a seat, pouring the coffee. 'We'll go through the questions, shall we? While Anya's keeping Gabriel amused.'

Maya's questions were searching, but her gentle tone and her smile made them feel less challenging. Before long, they were simply talking, and Raina felt herself relax.

'She manages very well...' Gabriel's occasional murmured interjections were all very much to the point. He was obviously listening, even if it seemed that his attention was solely focussed on Anya.

'Yes, she does. But as a doctor, I know that many people with limb differences suffer from overuse issues in the long term. And I want to give her as many choices as I can.'

'What choices?' Maya asked.

'I don't know. She'll tell me what she wants to do, when she wants to do it. I just want to be able to respond to that. If it takes time and money to make custom prosthetics, then that doesn't allow her to try things out, the way that most children can.'

'Good point.' Gabriel flashed Raina a smile, and then went back to the structure that he and Anya had built.

Alistair had been at a loss all morning. He'd decided that he should make himself scarce during Raina and Anya's interview, and had gone upstairs to spend some time with the development team for the prosthetics project. But he'd struggled to hear everything that was said and keep up with the exchange of ideas. He'd ended up sitting in the corner, drinking coffee and thinking about Raina.

If Gabriel and Maya decided that another child was a better fit for the project, then this would be his last chance to see her. She'd disappear again, a face in the crowd that he'd looked for time and time again, and never found. He'd often thought of her, the mental picture including the child that she'd always wanted, and this might be his only opportunity to see that reality.

It would take a little planning if he was to bump into her on her way out. Hanging around in Reception bore no fruit, so he decided that he might return to his office, where he was sure to at least catch a glimpse of Raina and Anya when they left. As he walked towards it, he saw the door of Gabriel's office open, and the beat of his heart started suddenly to thunder in his ears.

Then he saw Raina, joining Maya in the doorway. She was dressed in a pair of dark slacks with a cream blouse, the perfect choice for an informal interview. She looked stunning. A little girl in a blue and white summer dress ran to her side and Gabriel appeared, shaking Raina's hand and then looking down as the child tugged at his sleeve.

Alistair held his breath, unable to move. Gabriel bent towards the child, and she planted a kiss on his cheek. Maya laughed, obviously making a joke of it, and Gabriel stood up again, grinning helplessly. Fierce jealousy wound its fingers around Alistair's heart and squeezed hard. It should have been him…

No. It shouldn't have been him. He'd already decided that he'd make just as bad a father as his own father had been, and that Raina would be happier with someone else.

Suddenly he didn't want to see Raina after all, not with the daughter that looked so like her. But it was too late. Gabriel had looked up and was signalling for him to come over and join them. There was no way out, and Alistair forced himself to smile as he walked across the office.

The interview had gone well. Raina had said what she wanted to say, and answered all of Maya's questions. She'd seen Gabriel nod a few times, and although he hadn't said much perhaps he would support her candidacy. If Anya didn't get a place on the project, then at least Raina could tell herself that she'd done her best.

And then... Alistair. Standing at the far end of the office as she said her goodbyes to Gabriel and Maya. It would have been a great deal better if she hadn't known him so well, because then she would have mistaken the smile he was wearing as one of surprised welcome.

'Raina. It's good to see you again.' The way his thumb tapped against the side of the tablet computer he carried gave him away. Something was bothering Alistair.

'And you. This is Anya.'

Anya was looking up at him, curious about this new person.

'Yes, of course. Hello, Anya.'

He could barely look at her. Alistair had shown more genuine concern for the child he'd pulled out of the Thames than he did for Anya. Raina bit back the temptation to shake him and demand that he do a little more than just acknowledge her daughter's presence.

Maybe he was just trying a bit too hard to step back. No decisions had been made yet, and he didn't want to betray any bias. She shouldn't either, which meant that the swelling around the cut on his face and the consequent bruising under his eye was out of bounds as a topic of conversation.

'Your eye's looking better, Alistair. How does it feel now?' Maya asked the question that Raina didn't dare to.

'Much better, thanks. The antibiotics that Gabriel prescribed have done the trick.' Alistair had the grace to look a little sheepish. 'I really should have listened to Raina.'

'Yes, you should...' The words escaped her lips before Raina had a chance to swallow them down, and Anya looked up at Alistair.

'Naughty Alistair.'

It could have been worse. At least Anya's words hadn't come right out of the blue, and Gabriel chuckled.

'That's right, Anya. My thoughts exactly.' Gabriel ignored Alistair's glare and Raina's reddening cheeks.

'We should be going.' She found Anya's hand, gripping it tight. 'Thank you so much for your time. I really appreciate your seeing us.'

'It's been a pleasure. Thank you for letting me play with your bricks, Anya.'

'You're welcome,' Anya piped up again, and this time everyone smiled.

Handshakes were exchanged, and Raina hurried Anya away, leaving Gabriel and Maya to follow Alistair into the office next door to Gabriel's. She was trembling, Alistair's quiet words when they'd parted had made her heart beat even faster than it had when she'd first seen him. *Good luck.* If that meant what she thought it did, then the awkwardness of their meeting was something that could be set aside.

It was Gabriel and Maya's decision whether Anya would be accepted onto the project, but Alistair had made his own position very clear.

CHAPTER FOUR

IT HAD BEEN plain to Alistair and he'd wondered whether Gabriel and Maya would see it too. The pilot scheme wasn't just a matter of selecting the right children, it was a case of selecting the right parents, who could report back on their children's progress and help the team make the required adjustments to their procedures. Anya and Raina were both perfect.

Maya and Gabriel followed him into his office and Maya sat down, while Gabriel leaned across the desk to look at his eye. Alistair batted his hand away.

'It's improving. I know I should have mentioned it to you sooner.'

Gabriel grinned. 'Yes, you should. Next time you decide on any heroics, you might like to try following the advice of the doctor who was on the scene.'

Alistair glared at Gabriel and he backed off. This was the way it always was between them, they were firm friends whose disagreements were entirely without rancour. It was a synergy between two very different personalities, which brought the best out in both.

'I've made my mind up.' Maya ignored the glares in much the same way that everyone else in the office did. 'I think Raina could make a huge contribution to the project and she seems committed to doing so.'

Gabriel nodded. 'I agree. Anya's one of the best candidates we've seen as well.'

'And that's the decision?' Alistair didn't want to say anything to influence his colleagues.

Maya glanced at Gabriel and he nodded. 'Yes, let's make it official. We'll offer Anya a place on the project. We have two other children whose families have already accepted a place and you were going to speak with another three, Alistair.'

'I've done that. Two would like to take part, and Sam Ross's parents would like to wait. He's going into hospital for an operation, and he needs to be fully recovered before we can work with him to his best advantage.'

'So that's five in all. The Dream Team can handle six,' Gabriel said, pursing his lips.

'Yes, but I'd rather have fewer children and be sure that they're exactly right for the project.' Alistair's heart was beginning to beat a little faster. Everything he'd worked so hard for was becoming a reality.

Maya nodded. 'That sounds good to me. And…you're sure about working so closely with your ex-wife? If you have any concerns, I'd be happy to take Anya on myself.'

'I'm sure.' Alistair had made his mind up about this. 'Raina only wants the best for Anya and so do I. Everything else is secondary, and we can deal with it.'

Gabriel raised his eyebrows but said nothing. Clearly he had the same doubts as Alistair did and he was going to do exactly the same with them. Put them to the back of his mind and make this work, whatever the cost.

'Well, I'll be there if you need me. I think it would be a very good idea to invite Raina to the conference you're organising as well.'

Alistair frowned. It was a very good idea, but it meant treating Raina differently from the other parents on the project, and he'd promised he wouldn't do that.

'We've earmarked one day for the attending

charities to exhibit their own work, and compare it with what the others are doing. Gabriel and I were considering asking all the parents if they'd like to come down for that.'

'But Raina's a doctor,' Maya reminded him gently. 'I think that she could contribute a great deal to the discussion over the whole of the three days. She has practical experience as a mother as well as understanding the medical issues.'

Alistair glanced in Gabriel's direction. This was turning out to be more difficult than he'd thought, and he'd really rather not make the decision.

'I think we should ask her. I know you don't want to give Raina any special treatment, Alistair, but her qualifications as a doctor and a mother mean that she can make a valuable contribution. Excluding her on the basis of your previous relationship would be overcompensating.'

All the same, Alistair still didn't feel comfortable about asking Raina to come. 'You'll mention it to her, then? When you do Anya's initial medical examination?'

Gabriel shrugged. 'Yes, I'll ask her to save

the date. It's only a little more than a month away now.'

'That's agreed, then.' Maya cut the conversation short with a determined smile. 'I have two hours before I need to get back for my clinic. Which one of you is going to tempt me away from canteen sandwiches?'

Alistair chuckled, getting to his feet. Lunch was an altogether easier topic of conversation. 'I'll go over to the coffee shop and get something. There are a couple of things I'd like to discuss with you while you're here, Maya...'

Even the lunchtime chatter and the blaring music of the coffee shop couldn't dent Alistair's mood. Suddenly he felt useful again. He'd taken time off work when the SSHL had struck, and had come back to find that Gabriel's new wife, Clara, had been helping out. She was better than good for Gabriel, and his friend was happier than Alistair had ever seen him. Clara grounded his creative volatile nature, helping him to direct his energies in the right way. That had once been Alistair's role, and although he was pleased to share it, and delighted to find the office running smoothly without him, he couldn't help but wonder whether he was really needed as much as he'd thought he was.

His value seemed to have diminished over the whole spectrum of his work. People were getting on with their business, making telephone calls that he couldn't hear and saying things that he only half understood. By the time he could put all the pieces together, the chance to reply was gone and there was another puzzling snatch of conversation to work on. He'd been running at full tilt just to keep up.

But now the project that Gabriel had encouraged him to concentrate on was coming to fruition. And Raina was going to be a part of it. Alistair couldn't work out which of those things he was most looking forward to, and he didn't question himself too closely on that score. Gabriel had been right, he'd needed a challenge. And that was exactly what he was going to get.

Raina was wearing a pair of dark slim-leg trousers and a neat white shirt. In Alistair's experience, she had always dressed for effect, and the effect here was businesslike. Anya, on the other hand, wore a red and white sleeveless sundress. No attempt had been made to cover her arms and the little girl's inquisitive air showed no sign of self-consciousness. She'd never been told that she was anything other than perfect, and Alistair knew from his dealings with other mothers that that was an achievement on Raina's part.

He met her at the door to his office, putting on a smile. 'Hi, Anya.'

'Hello. Mummy says I mustn't call you *Naughty* Alistair.' The little girl regarded him solemnly and a sudden rush of tenderness filled Alistair's heart. He glanced up at Raina, and saw her cheeks flushing red.

'So what *would* you like to call me?'

Anya shrugged, letting go of Raina's hand and reaching for the plastic food bag that her mother carried. 'I made you a cake.'

'We've been baking.' Raina was clearly relieved that her daughter had changed the subject. 'Anya helped with the icing.'

Alistair took the bag, opening it and unwrapping the greaseproof paper inside. 'A cinnamon bun. Thank you, Anya.'

'That's all right. We've got lots more.' Anya

was peering past him into his office, and Alistair stepped back. Raina mouthed, *Sorry*, and Alistair shook his head. No apologies needed.

'Gabriel's given you the details of our conference?' Alistair supposed he'd better mention it.

'Yes, we talked about it when he did Anya's medical examination. It sounds really interesting. I'd love to come.'

Alistair had been hoping that Raina might find an excuse not to attend. Conferences had a way of throwing people together, and he wasn't quite comfortable with being thrown together with Raina yet. But he'd worry about that when the time came.

'Good. Gabriel's prescribed a myolectric prosthesis for Anya. Do you have any questions about that?'

'No, but...' Raina pressed her lips together. 'A myolectric prosthesis would give her the ability to move the fingers and take on more complex manual tasks, but it takes a bit of perseverance in learning how to use the muscles of the arm to control it.'

Alistair sat down behind his desk, putting the bun down next to the phone and waving Raina to a seat. This all seemed sufficiently business-like. Raina had taken a rag doll from her bag, giving it to Anya, and the little girl had meandered over to the easy chairs that stood at the other end of the office and climbed into one, sitting the doll in her lap and whispering to it. Alistair couldn't hear what she was saying, but presumably Raina could and was happy to let her play alone for a while.

'And you have a concern about that?'

'I don't know. Maybe. A fixed or semi-flexible prosthesis is less expensive to produce and more durable, so it may be a more practical option to start with. Particularly if we're not sure what Anya's reaction is going to be yet.'

Alistair nodded. 'We agreed that this was all about presenting Anya with choices. This project is about dreams and possibilities, so tell me which ones you want her to have...'

Raina's wry smile told Alistair that she didn't deal much in the currency of dreams. The last few years had forced her to deal with harsh reality.

'The myolectric hand.' She had one dream left, at least.

'Then that's what we'll work towards. Let

us worry about the expense and the difficulty, your job is to support your daughter.'

That would be a challenge for Raina. It had never been all that easy for her to let go and allow someone else to deal with a problem. But this was what she'd signed up to do when she'd accepted a place on the project, and Alistair couldn't imagine that Gabriel hadn't made that crystal clear to her.

Her gaze searched his face, and he wondered what she saw. Then suddenly she nodded. 'Yes. Thank you.'

That was the hard part over. Now Alistair could get on with what he had planned for the day.

'In that case, let's give her an idea first of how we can make the things she imagines into a reality. I thought we'd spend some time with our development team for starters—we call them the Dream Team.'

Raina smiled, looking round at her daughter. 'That sounds like a great idea.'

The little girl was still deep in conversation with her doll. Every time Alistair looked at Anya, a special kind of pain tugged at his heart. But it would fade in time, and until then he'd have to ignore it.

He rose, picking up the box that contained his hearing aid and stuffing it into his pocket. Raina called Anya, telling her that they had to go now, then paused suddenly.

'Is that your new hearing aid?'

'Yes. I only got it a few days ago, and I have to wear it for two hours a day for starters.'

'I seem to remember from my time in audiology that it's *at least* two hours a day.' Raina had done a turn in the hospital's audiology department when she'd been training, and it was typical of her that she forgot nothing. Everyone else in the office, Gabriel included, just took his word for it.

'Yes. Now you mention it…' Alistair took the box from his pocket, taking out the hearing aid, aware that Anya was regarding him solemnly.

'What's that?'

'It's…um…' He shot Raina a questioning look. Alistair wasn't at all sure how to explain a hearing aid to a three-year-old. Or why a child with presumably perfect hearing would even want to know.

'That's Alistair's hearing aid, sweetie.' Raina came to his rescue. 'Alistair's ear has stopped working, and his hearing aid helps him to hear everything we say to him.'

She said the words as if she was describing a miracle. That had been Alistair's first thought, until the odd sounds that the hearing aid produced had set in, and it had felt more like an instrument of torture. Nothing sounded quite the way he remembered it. But Anya believed in the miracle, and her eyes were as round as saucers.

He put the earpiece into his ear, adjusting the back to sit neatly behind it. Suddenly the muted sounds around him sprang into sharp, almost agonising focus, but Alistair smiled all the same.

'Did you make it?' Anya had obviously been told a little about what she was here for.

'No, I didn't make it. But we make lots of other things. Would you like to come and see them?' Today was all about showing Anya that science could help people, and maybe he should take heed of the lesson too.

* * *

Pre-meeting nerves hadn't covered it. It was more a matter of feeling sick to her stomach, feeling her body stiff with tension. This meant so much for Anya. And Raina was determined not to admit that it meant a great deal to *her* that it was Alistair who would be taking her case.

He was committed to this project, and when Alistair committed himself to something he rarely failed. He would undoubtedly do his very best for Anya, and that was what Raina wanted. He'd be professional, hiding whatever emotion he had about the situation, because that was what Alistair did supremely well.

He ushered them upstairs, walking into a large office and introducing everyone. Kaia, Ben and Alfie had clearly taken control of their environment, making it look something like a teenager's bedroom. Kaia was the most outgoing of the three, getting up from behind the large computer screen on her desk and coming over to chat. She wore a filmy pinafore dress over a T-shirt, with sneakers, and looked casual and cool.

'I've got some bricks, Anya. I made them

myself.' Kaia bent down to speak to Anya. 'Would you like to come and see?'

Anya nodded, looking up at Raina. 'Yes, that's all right. Go with Kaia.' She watched them walk over to a purple sofa in the corner of the room. There was a pile of bricks on the coffee table in front of it, and when Anya picked one up it caught the light, sparkling brightly. It seemed that she was about to get a fun idea of what the 3D printer could produce.

Alistair shot her a smile and sauntered over to Ben's workstation, peering over his shoulder. Ben had taken the least notice of them, acknowledging their presence only with a nod and the raising of his hand, before going back to the two computer screens in front of him.

'Do you want something?'

Alistair shrugged. 'No. Just taking an interest. And pretending I know what on earth that is.' He nodded at the screen.

Ben responded with a half-smile. These three were clearly young and talented and it seemed that Ben was working on the cutting edge of something that everyone else only barely understood. Alistair had the difficult job of giving them direction and keeping their feet on the ground.

'It's the mechanism for closing the hand. It wasn't exactly right.'

Alfie chuckled. 'Yeah. Make a fist, Alistair. Ben's been driving everyone crazy...'

Ben frowned. 'Because making a fist isn't just making a fist. If you wanted to punch me, then your thumb would be in a very different place from if you wanted to pick something up.'

Alfie rolled his eyes, in a clear indication that he already wanted to punch Ben. Alistair gave that easygoing grin that could smooth over the most troubled waters.

'Suppose we resort to real-world expectations?'

Ben's shrug in reply indicated that real-world expectations weren't his thing. No wonder they called this the Dream Team. Raina reckoned that it took a bit of work to keep their feet touching the ground even part of the time.

'What are your thoughts, Raina?' A smile hovered on Alistair's lips.

'Well...' Raina decided that she should at least recognise Ben's way of thinking. 'Most parents would say they wanted their children to pick things up rather than punch them. And I have seen instances of children using their prostheses as a weapon, they put them on only when they want to hit out at something. So I think that the arm should work like a tool and not a weapon.'

'Yeah, form and function. I get it.' He nodded and looked back at his screen, muttering under his breath, *'Finally. Some sanity.'*

Alistair chuckled. 'I heard that, Ben. I've got my hearing aid in.'

Ben was already lost in his thoughts. 'You know one day we'll be able to make a limb that can feel. Assess temperature and texture…' He smiled suddenly, as if the impossible was just something that hadn't happened yet.

'One day. Not today. At the moment we're finding out what's going to be best for Anya…' Alistair raised one eyebrow, as if this was a conversation he'd already had with Ben.

'Yeah, okay. Well, I'll need to see our subject pick up a range of things. In a controlled environment.'

'Forget it, Ben,' Alistair replied. 'This is the real world, and you can't ask a three-year-old to pick up objects of varying weight and size and put them back down again a hundred times, while you watch her do it. And her name's Anya.'

'Uh. Yes, sorry.' Ben flashed Raina an apologetic look and went straight back to his screen.

'What about getting Anya to draw something, and then rendering it up as a 3D model and printing it. Then you can watch her play with it and see how she handles it.' Alistair had hit on a middle way, glancing from Raina to Ben to see if it met with approval from both of them.

'That would be great, she'd love that. And it would be a way of showing her that what she imagines can be made real.' Raina hesitated. 'If it's not going to take up too much of Ben's time.'

Alistair shook his head. 'This project is all about finding out what works. None of that is going to be a waste of time.'

Ben nodded. 'What are we going to print?'

'Anything she likes. As Raina said, it's about showing her that *her* dreams can be made into reality.'

'I could do a velociraptor.' Ben's face lit up.

'They're fascinating creatures. Computer modelling shows that they may have used their tails as balance mechanisms…'

'She doesn't know what a velociraptor is, but she loves dinosaurs.' Raina ventured a compromise.

'Great.' Alistair beamed. 'So we'll ask her to draw a dinosaur and Ben can make whatever *small* adjustments are needed to stop it from falling flat on its face. I think we're all on the same page now.'

Somehow they were. Alistair's ability to negotiate between two entirely different points of view had never been in doubt. It was *his* point of view that had eluded Raina. But his private thoughts were no longer any of her concern.

His head was buzzing, and a series of loud, inexplicable noises seemed to be coming from somewhere. When Alistair looked around the room, it turned out to be the hiss of the coffee machine. At this rate it was going to be a miracle if he managed to keep track of a three-year-old, an ex-wife and three designers who were gifted but didn't have the practical experience to turn their ideas into workable solutions.

At least he was having no difficulty hearing what Raina said. He wondered whether that was because he seemed to be acutely aware of every move she made, and decided that it was because she was making it easy for him to hear her. This project mattered as much to her as it did to him, and communication was the key.

But since everyone seemed to be communicating pretty well without him, he retired to the corner of the room, taking out his hearing aid. It was the aural equivalent of someone suddenly putting a bag over his head, and everything seemed suddenly muffled and indistinct. But at least he wasn't jumping all the time.

'Going to put that back on?' Somehow Raina managed to speak in a way that he could hear, and yet at the same time make their conversation private. How did she do that?

'Um… Not at the moment. I think that the audiologist must have adjusted it incorrectly, everything seems very distorted.' Alistair pulled open the battery compartment to switch the hearing aid off, and put it into his pocket.

'It's going to sound distorted. If anything, that means they've got it right, because you're hearing things that you haven't heard for the last few months. Your brain just needs a bit of time to catch up and learn how to process those sounds again.'

'The audiologist did mention that. But I don't think this can be right. I feel constantly on edge with it.'

'Of course you do. We instinctively react to sounds we don't recognise and block out the ones we do if they're of no importance to us.'

When Raina reminded him of that well-understood fact, everything seemed a bit better. Warmer and full of promise, tempering the harsh, brittle sounds that he felt overwhelmed by at times.

'I suppose that asking a three-year-old to get to grips with a new arm, when I've got my hearing aid in my pocket is… I should practise what I preach a little more.'

Raina shrugged. 'I'm sure that Anya will need a bit of coaxing, too. Kaia seems to be making a good job of that.' She nodded over to where Kaia had lifted Anya up to see through the partition window, into the room where the 3D printer was housed. Alistair had reckoned that sparkly plastic bricks might catch Anya's attention and they were small enough that they didn't take too long to print.

'And that's what you're doing? Coaxing me?' Alistair rather wished that she would.

She smiled suddenly, stepping closer. Alistair caught a trace of her scent and suddenly his whole body was taking notice of Raina. 'Perhaps I can get Ben to make you a sparkly cover for your earpiece.'

Alistair took the hearing aid from his pocket and put it back into his ear. 'Don't do that. He'll be wanting to incorporate something useful. GPS tracking probably to give them advanced warning of when I'm on my way up here.'

'That *would* be useful.' Raina seemed to suddenly realise that the conversation had slipped into familiarity and that they were standing very close. Almost touching. Her cheeks flushed and she stepped back. Alistair wondered whether he should apologise and decided that would only make things even more awkward.

Alistair cleared his throat, trying to dislodge the lump that had formed, forcing his thoughts back to the present and the task in hand. 'So… practically speaking, we can fit Anya with a new prosthetic very easily. Our real difficulty is going to be in showing her what benefits it might give her.'

'You have some ideas about that?' Raina looked up at him, and when Alistair saw the trust in her dark eyes he almost turned away in shame. He'd done so little to deserve her trust, but maybe he could change that. If he paid the debt that he owed her, maybe he could bring himself to move on with his life.

'Yes, I have some ideas. But first I'd like Anya to spend some more time up here. Kaia's got some great ideas for fun things to make, and I'm hoping that if Anya gets involved with that process, she'll feel that making her a prosthetic is just another fun thing that we can do.'

'That sounds wonderful. When would you like us to come back?'

'As often as you like. Kaia's working with one of the other children on the project in the mornings, but she's set aside her afternoons for Anya.'

'Tomorrow?' Raina's face lit up in a smile, and Alistair couldn't help feeling that this was the reason he'd got out of bed this morning.

'Tomorrow would be great.'

CHAPTER FIVE

THE DREAM TEAM had walked the extra mile and then one more for Anya. Ben had made a dinosaur for her, which was a direct replica of one that the little girl had drawn, right down to the smile on its face. The bricks took a shorter time to print, and Anya was beginning to understand that anything that she or the Dream Team could imagine might emerge from the 'magic printer'.

The two offices at the far end of the main office were both beginning to look more and more like playrooms. Gabriel's was all his own work, and when he was in the office he seemed to add something more every day to the pile of toys that he was assessing for suitability for the twins that he and his wife Clara were expecting.

'He'll get over it.' Alistair had smilingly dismissed his friend's enthusiasm. 'Gabriel never does anything by halves.'

Raina shook her head, trying to smile. Gabriel was never going to get over it, and that was exactly as it should be. He'd given his heart already, and Raina knew from her own experience that there was never going to be a time when he got it back.

Alistair's office was a little more focussed. Five boxes, one of which bore Anya's name and contained her bricks and the dinosaur. Whenever they visited, he carried the box upstairs, staying for a while to observe the sessions with Kaia.

'She's naturally right-handed?' Alistair and Raina had left Anya with Kaia, and gone back downstairs to talk.

'As far as I know. Both Andrew and Theresa were right handed, and statistically it's much more likely. She was too young when the accident happened to have already shown any preference.'

Alistair nodded, recording her answer on his laptop. He'd been taking notes of everything and they'd form a good record of Anya's development and progress. Probably nothing like the record that was engraved on Raina's heart, but...that wasn't the aim, here.

'There is evidence that when older people lose their dominant hand, the brain compensates.' He mulled the question over for a moment. 'Have you ever seen any evidence that she experiences phantom feelings or pain?'

'No. Not as far as I know. She never talks about her *other* hand. Obviously she's noticed that most people have two, but it's normal for her to just have one.'

Alistair nodded. 'The research is inconclusive, but that would be in line with what's generally recognised to be the case.'

'Yeah. I seem to remember...' Raina shook her head.

'Remember what?' Alistair stopped typing and shot her a questioning look.

'Nothing. Just that I read up about all of this and...to be honest, most of what I read is a bit of a blur.' She shrugged guiltily.

Alistair leaned back in his chair, his face softening suddenly. 'Of course it is. You were grieving and learning to take care of a child. You must have been exhausted.'

It was the first time they'd touched on her feelings. This had been all about Anya, and how she felt. Having Alistair ask about what *she* felt was more uncomfortable and raised questions she'd rather not answer.

'Yeah. I suppose so.'

'Have you talked to anyone about this?'

Had she *talked?* Alistair had barely been there to talk to when she'd lost their baby. That had been one of the things that had torn them apart. Raina bit back the urge to snap at him.

'Yes.' That would do. He didn't need to know where she'd found support from, he just needed to know any particulars that referred to Anya's case. Wanting to tell him how hard that first year had been wasn't going to make him understand that any better.

'Right. Good.' Thankfully Alistair didn't write that down.

'What about *your* feelings, Alistair?' The words had been on the tip of her tongue for days now, and they slipped out before Raina could stop them.

'My feelings?' He gave her an innocent look, which didn't wash for a minute. Alistair had been friendly and kind, making sure that Anya had everything she needed. But he'd never played with her, and seldom even spoke to her unless he had to.

Raina swallowed hard. 'I just meant… You must have them.'

'Yes. I do.' His face was impassive. He was never going to change, and Raina had to accept that. A tear rolled down her face, and she wiped it away. She didn't want Alistair to see her crying.

'Come with me.' He stood, ushering her out of his office, past the desks outside. Raina followed him up the stairs, past the Dream Team's office, and into the conference room.

'Let's talk.' Alistair had flipped the sign outside to indicate there was a meeting in progress, and he closed the door.

'Okay.' Raina's knees were beginning to shake and she sat down. 'What do you want to talk about?'

'Whatever it is you're not saying to me, you can go ahead and say it. Anya's place on the project is secure and inviolable. Nothing you could possibly do or say can change that.'

'We said…we *promised* that we wouldn't let our relationship get in the way of the work, Alistair.'

'Yes, we did. And you're going back on that promise.'

'Me?' The anger that Raina had been biting back for days suddenly broke loose. '*I've* gone back on it? You're heading this project and...'

Raina was almost breathless with rage. Maybe she should have told him that she could never have another child. He'd understand then why she was so angry. But it was too late now, and it was buried too deep. Raina had hidden that pain from everyone.

'And...?'

'And you can hardly even look at her.'

Alistair strode to a seat opposite hers, flinging himself down in it. 'Do you actually think that I don't feel anything when I see Anya? That I don't think about the child we lost?'

The vehemence in his voice was shocking. Almost as shocking as the way Raina felt. 'But you never really wanted a child, Alistair. You talked about not being ready...'

'I *wasn't* ready. That doesn't mean that I didn't want our child, and that I didn't grieve for it. But you were physically and mentally traumatised, you needed care.'

'I needed to know how you felt. I didn't want to go through it on my own.' Raina jumped to her feet and started to pace. Alistair rose, catching her by the shoulders.

'No, Raina. You don't do that to me. Whatever you say, you have to say it to my face, or I won't hear you properly.'

Alistair had never asked for any concession to be made for his deafness. And now he was demanding one. If he could make that step, then the least that Raina could do was to hear him.

'How *did* you feel, Alistair?'

'You want to know, all of a sudden? You were the one who left me, Raina.'

The barb hit home. She'd left her wedding and engagement rings on the kitchen table and just walked away. Two weeks later she'd filed for divorce.

'I know. And I know that must have hurt, but you were spending so much time at work that there was no opportunity to talk.' Raina tried to keep her voice steady.

His face darkened. 'I felt guilty. That I wasn't there for you when you lost the baby.'

She'd called him, leaving message after message, but Alistair had been at work and he'd switched his phone off. Hurt wouldn't allow her to admit how much she'd needed him.

'There was nothing you could have done.'

'That was just the problem, wasn't it?' Alistair turned suddenly, as if he didn't want to hear any more of this. 'There was never anything that I could do.'

Maybe she hadn't given him much opportunity to feel anything, Raina's own grief had seemed to fill every part of the space around her. Maybe she *had* pushed him away, but that was only because she'd known that Alistair had already been doing what he always did when something was too difficult, and spending every waking hour at work.

He had to hear this. Raina reached for his arm, pulling him round to face her again. 'I'm listening now.'

Alistair's gaze searched her face. Cold and hard, as if he was protecting himself from something. 'When you lost the baby I was heartbroken. Is that what you want to hear?'

She knew he was telling the truth. She could see his pain. As the nagging doubt about whether he'd ever wanted the child they'd lost dissolved, a weight seemed to lift from Raina's heart.

'It's what I *needed* to hear…' She could feel tears spilling down her cheeks. Raina had thought that the silence between them had destroyed everything, but this cathartic spark had somehow ignited life into a relationship she'd thought was long dead.

Alistair wound his arms around her shoulders suddenly, pulling her close. As she sobbed against his chest, she could feel his breath catch with emotion.

'We can't let this come between us. We're both angry, but we have to put that aside for Anya's sake…' Finally he spoke.

Raina rubbed at her eyes with her hand. He wouldn't hear her if she mumbled into his chest, but when she looked up at Alistair it was hard not to see the man she'd wanted to share her life with. The one she'd wanted to kiss…

No. There were good reasons why it was over and, however much they voiced their differences, neither of them would ever change.

'We promised that we would. It's harder than I thought, though.'

Alistair nodded. 'I can't pretend that being

with Anya doesn't remind me of the child we lost, any more than I can keep pretending that I'll wake up tomorrow and be able to hear again. Those things are gone now.' He let her go, stepping back.

'It's not easy. I asked a lot of you when I applied for the project, and you could be forgiven for taking your time.'

He shot her a reproachful look. 'Don't give up on me now. You need to stop trying to be so nice to me, and start telling me what you think. I can't do this on my own.'

'You want me to be the Wicked Witch, do you?' She raised her eyebrows and as Alistair smiled, the atmosphere between them lifted.

'No. I just want your opinions. I know you have them…'

'Are you calling me opinionated? I could say the same about you.'

Alistair chuckled. It seemed that they'd found a way to make this work after all. Not without some pain, but the gain had been worth it. 'You want the last word on that? I could come up with some compelling arguments.'

Raina grinned. 'Don't waste your time. I'm having the last word.'

* * *

'Right, then, Edward.' Alistair arranged the teddy bear carefully next to the small table and chair that was set up in the corner of his office for Anya. 'Let's see how you manage...'

He pressed Edward's arm, and the bear's small prosthetic fingers closed. Perfect. Pressing on the other side made them open again. It wasn't quite the same mechanism that Anya would use to control her prosthetic hand, but hopefully it made the connection between Edward's arm and the new hand clear.

Kaia and Ben had produced this smaller prosthetic, and it had been down to Alistair to perform the surgery on the teddy bear. When he'd removed the lower part of Edward's arm and stitched the opening closed, Alistair had felt uncharacteristically squeamish. Maybe it was the eyes, looking at him unblinkingly as he completed the procedure.

Raina and Anya would be coming again this afternoon, and Alistair was having a hard time keeping himself from smiling at the thought. In the last two weeks, he'd begun to develop a relationship with Anya, and found that the more he did so, the less he compared her with the child he and Raina had lost. And under Raina's watchful eye he'd begun to accept that he needed a hearing aid, and put into practice all the little techniques that allowed him to hear better.

It was a hot day, and when Alistair looked up from his labours and saw Raina in the outer office she was wearing a blue-patterned dress, made from material that looked as if it would be soft and thin if he were to touch it. Everything she'd worn in the last two weeks had somehow imprinted itself on his memory. The dark, formal trousers. A more casual pair of cargo pants. Stiff shirts had given way to pretty tops and T-shirts. And now a dress.

It was tempting to feel that Raina's choice of outfit might be reflecting her growing confidence about the situation, and with it their relationship. But Alistair didn't have the words to explore that and instead he greeted them both with a smile.

'I've got…a new friend.' Alistair gestured towards Edward, and saw Raina's eyes widen. Anya was a little less impressed.

'Who is it?'

'He doesn't have a name.' *Edward* was purely

between Alistair and the bear. 'Do you want to give him one?'

Anya thought for a moment. 'No.'

'Okay. How about Edward, then?' Anya didn't seem to mind much one way or the other, and Alistair decided he should keep trying. 'Would you like to see what he can do?'

He walked over to the bear and squeezed his arm, and the small fingers closed, then opened again. Then Alistair moved his arm and squeezed, making Edward pick up one of the bricks from Anya's table.

'That's so clever!' It wasn't clear whether Raina's smiling exclamation was for Anya's benefit or his, but Alistair grinned up at her, shivering as he met her gaze.

Anya walked over to Edward, whispering into his ear, and Alistair decided to leave her to it, retreating to one of the easy chairs that surrounded the coffee table. She was interested, at least. Whatever it was that Anya was saying to Edward, and he was saying back, appeared to be serious business.

'He doesn't like it, Mummy.' Finally Anya turned, her brow furrowed.

'Doesn't like what, sweetie?' Raina joined her daughter, kneeling down next to her.

'That.' Anya swatted the prosthetic arm. 'Take it off.'

'But look, Anya. It helps him to pick the bricks up.' Raina pressed Edward's arm, finding the place that operated the hand. She took a shot at opening and closing the fingers and then tried to pick up a brick.

'No, Mummy…' Anya seemed about to burst into tears, and Raina looked equally crestfallen. Alistair got to his feet quickly.

'That's okay, Anya. It's okay, we'll take it off if Edward doesn't like it. He doesn't have to wear it if he doesn't want to.' He slid the prosthetic off Edward's arm and put it on his desk, out of Anya's reach. Maybe it would assume the importance of everything else on his desk in Anya's mind. Something to be reached for and played with when she thought he wasn't looking.

'He wants to draw.'

'That sounds like a good idea.' Alistair picked up the bear, putting him into Anya's lap and pushing her crayons towards her.

The picture was drawn, admired and pinned

on the wall and then Alistair suggested that they go upstairs to the Dream Team's office. Raina was quiet, her thoughts seeming to bother her, and when she asked Kaia to watch Anya while she slipped out for a moment, Alistair followed her.

She wasn't in his office, and the receptionist said that she'd seen Raina go out. When Alistair opened the front door and looked outside, he could see a splash of blue amongst the greenery in the square across the road.

He felt in his pocket for change, making sure he had enough. Then he walked quickly to the coffee shop on the corner and made his way back to the square. She was sitting on a bench, staring straight in front of her, and didn't move when Alistair sat down beside her.

'Here.' He passed her the coffee.

'Thanks.' She didn't look at him, but she took the cup. They sat in silence for a while, and Alistair sipped his drink.

'What's bugging you?' He knew, but this seemed a good place to start the conversation.

Raina sighed. 'The teddy bear...it's so beautiful. It was a great idea and she rejected it.'

'That's okay. We're not expecting everything

to work for every child. Maybe Edward will have better luck with someone else.'

'Do you think she'll ever be ready to at least try a prosthetic?'

Alistair shrugged. 'I don't know. I'm not going to give up on her, though. When we asked you and Anya to be part of the project we asked for a commitment from you, and we owe you a commitment in return.'

He owed it. But *'we'* was a far less dangerous thing to say, and it happened to be true. It was Gabriel and Maya who had chosen Anya for the project, and Gabriel was Anya's doctor.

She nodded slowly. 'I could still help with the other children. If you think I have something to offer…'

'I think you have a great deal to offer, and we'd be glad to have you help. And that might be the thing that works for Anya, if she sees you helping other kids with their prosthetics maybe she'll want to explore the idea for herself.'

He reached out, touching her on the back of her hand to make sure he had her attention. His head was buzzing from the tinnitus and the birds had chosen this moment to drown out his thoughts with their song. But when Raina looked at him everything else disappeared.

'Look, Raina. I made a promise, and it's got no time limit. If Anya accepts her prosthetic now, then well and good. If not then you can come back to me at any time, and we'll fit one then. *She* can come back to me, when she's old enough. Maybe Ben's right and by then we'll have something that's capable of things we can only dream about now.'

It felt like a commitment. No greater than the one he'd make to any other patient and their family maybe, but different. A binding promise that would stay with Anya all her life. Alistair tried not to think about the other binding promise he'd made to Raina. Their divorce had dissolved that, but somehow his heart had never quite accepted it.

'That's a very generous offer. I won't say no to it, for Anya's sake.'

Alistair felt a lump in his throat. Maybe this was all just phantom pain, the throbbing ache of something that had gone but that still hurt. His own hearing loss had made him re-alise that while it was possible to compensate for something that was lost, it was a learning process.

'We're not out of options yet. You just have to hang on in there while we work through them.'

'Thank you.'

'Don't thank me.' He held out his hand to her. 'Tell me it's a deal.'

Raina smiled suddenly, putting her hand in his. 'It's a deal.'

Letting go of her hand seemed like another loss. 'Now we have that settled, perhaps we'd better see what your daughter is doing to my development team. I don't want her leading them astray.'

Alistair held out his arm, wondering if Raina would take it. Ever since their explosive argument had cleared the air between them, she'd been careful to avoid any physical contact and Alistair had taken her lead on that. Somehow he needed it at the moment, though.

'They're perfectly capable of going astray without any help, aren't they?' She smiled, taking his arm, and Alistair suddenly realised he'd been holding his breath.

'Yes. Ben's been talking about making Anya

a robot. They seem to have struck up quite a friendship.'

He spun his empty cup into the bin, which stood next to the railings that enclosed the square. Raina shook her head in answer to his unspoken query, and took another sip of her coffee. They still had that. Raina's aim was uncertain at the best of times, and she'd always given her empty cup to him if the bin was more than a couple of yards away.

They climbed the steps to the front door of the office, and Raina let go of his arm as he ushered her inside.

'We'll find a way, Raina. We can get through to her. This is just a minor setback and we're bound to have some. But we'll get there.'

Raina turned to him, a trace of regret in her face. 'You're right. I shouldn't be so disappointed by every little setback.'

'It's natural. You're Anya's mother and you have a great deal invested in this. You're allowed to feel things.'

She laughed suddenly. 'Okay. I'll take care of the volatile mood swings, and you can be in charge of common sense.'

'It's a deal.' Now all Alistair had to do was to

think of something that would make the prosthetic more acceptable to Anya. And he needed to think quickly, for both Raina's and Anya's sakes.

CHAPTER SIX

'I'VE HAD AN IDEA.' Alistair didn't bother with a *Hello*, or an *Are you awake?* Raina rubbed her eyes, and sat up in bed. Anya would be awake soon, anyway.

'And it couldn't wait?' She stumbled out of bed. It had been a long time since she'd heard his voice this early in the morning, and it seemed somehow a little indecent to be talking to him while she was still in her pyjamas.

Raina rolled her eyes at her own foolishness. Alistair knew what she looked like in pyjamas.

'Sorry...sorry, you weren't asleep, were you?'

'No, not really. Hold on a minute.' Raina peered into Anya's room to see whether the phone had woken her, but her daughter was still slumbering peacefully. Tiptoeing down the stairs, she made for the kitchen and filled the coffee machine, switching it on.

'I'll have a cup of coffee in my hand in a moment. Don't throw anything too difficult at me before I've had my first mouthful.'

'Oh. You want me to ring back?'

'No, it's okay, tell me now. What's your idea?'

'I was thinking of a two-pronged attack—' Alistair stopped suddenly. 'I mean…well, I didn't mean we're actually going to attack Anya.'

Raina laughed. It was good to hear Alistair so enthusiastic about something that he'd spoken before carefully considering what he was about to say. 'That's okay. She's more than a match for you, Alistair.'

'Don't I know it. Well, the first prong of the…um…strategy, is that we hold off on giving her the myolectric prosthesis, and start her off with a semi flexible passive hand. That'll be lighter for her, and it'll help her to explore what she can do using two limbs instead of one. We can devise a few games for her, things like batting a ball back and forth.'

'That makes sense. And the second prong of this attack?'

'Is that she's seen too much of hospitals already. Being stuck all day in our office is probably a bit like visiting the hospital in her mind. Maybe she needs to be out and about or in her own home. Places where she wants to explore and where she feels more confident about being in control.'

Raina nodded. 'Yes, I think that's fair. The doctors and nurses at the hospital are always great with her, but she's always pleased when she gets home.' Raina picked her mug up, deciding that fetching the milk was too much of a distraction at the moment, and took a sip.

'So I'm wondering whether our spending time with Anya in your home for a whole day—a weekend even—would be something that might be of benefit. Would you consider that?'

Raina choked on her coffee. 'What, all of you?'

'No, just me. We don't want to overwhelm her. Are you all right?'

'Yes. Yes, my coffee went down the wrong way. Hold on…' Raina filled a glass and took a sip of water. The idea had its merits. The only drawback was that it was already proving tough enough to spend time with Alistair without noticing all the little things that had made her fall in love with him.

'It's very kind of you to offer, Alistair, but this is going to mean a lot of your time...'

'I'll do whatever it takes.'

Raina had no doubt of that. She'd do whatever it took as well, but Alistair had a wider group to consider. 'There aren't enough hours in the day for you to spend this much time with every child...'

'No, but this project is all about exploring possibilities. If this works for Anya, and I think it might, then we can look at the practicalities of offering it for other children.'

That made sense. And Alistair sounded so determined. He'd faced his own difficulties, and it was good to hear him reconnecting with his work so enthusiastically. Raina had to put her own qualms aside.

'Well...if you're sure. We'd love to have you here any time that suits you.'

'That's settled, then. How are you fixed for this weekend? Is there anything special she'd like to do?'

'Uh...just the normal things.' Raina decided she really needed coffee to face a weekend with Alistair, and took a mouthful from her cup. 'The same as you probably.'

He chuckled. 'I usually work...'

So nothing much had changed, then. 'Well, we usually go out somewhere on Saturday afternoon. The park sometimes, Anya likes to feed the ducks. We like going to new places and just taking a look around.'

'That sounds straightforward enough. How does ten o'clock suit you?'

Alistair clearly didn't have much idea of what it took to keep a three-year-old occupied for a whole day. Raina took another swig of her coffee.

'Ten o'clock's fine. We'll see you then.'

Alistair had been prepared to learn. And parents had told him how uncomfortable it was when people stared at their children, but he wasn't prepared for just how bad it felt.

They'd agreed that Alistair would come on Saturday and stay over until Sunday. He'd picked Raina and Anya up at ten, determined that it should be Raina's day out as well, and was glad to see her relax while he negotiated the London traffic, parking in Hyde Park. They strolled to the lake, and Raina took a plastic beaker from her bag, filling it with duck food and tucking it under Anya's arm so that she could use her hand to feed the ducks.

It was a gorgeous day, sun glinting on the water. Raina seemed relaxed and Anya was obviously having a good time, laughing and pointing at a white duck that came to the side of the water to eat the food that she threw.

'Mum… Look, that girl's only got one hand. *And* she's got food for the ducks.' A child's voice came from the pathway, and Alistair turned to see a young mother, bright red in the face and reprimanding her boy. Raina smiled at her.

'I'm so sorry…' The woman shot Raina an agonised look. Alistair glanced down at Anya, who seemed oblivious to anything but the ducks.

'That's okay. My daughter's name is Anya.'

The woman smiled. 'This is Tom.' Tom knew that he'd done something wrong and was hiding behind his mother's skirts.

'Would he like to come and feed the ducks with us?'

The woman hesitated for a moment and then smiled. 'Yes, he would. Thank you very much.'

Raina produced another plastic cup from her bag and tipped some food into it. Introductions were made, and the two children stood together feeding the ducks, their mothers holding onto them to stop them from falling into the water. When Anya's cup was empty, Tom held his in front of her so that she could reach into it.

Alistair watched as the two mothers chatted a little, and then Tom and his mum both said goodbye to Anya. Raina caught her hand, suggesting that they try some of the ducks a little further up, and Alistair fell into step beside them as they strolled along the path that ran alongside the lake.

'Nicely done.' Alistair wouldn't have known what to do. The urge to find some way to defend Anya from the looks that some of the people walking by the lake had given her had left him shaken.

Raina shrugged. 'People look. Some are really rude and you can't do anything about them... But most of the time it's just people being human.' She sighed. 'My best defence is to try to start up a dialogue. Most people are nice. They just don't know what to say.'

'Does she notice?' Anya's attention was on a pair of swans swimming gracefully along the far side of the lake, and she seemed completely oblivious of anything else.

'She doesn't like it if people just stare. I usually smile and people either look away or smile back. She told a woman to go away once.'

'Yeah? What happened?'

'Oh, she came up to me, wanting to know what had happened and whether Anya had been born like that. I was really taken aback, and…it wasn't that good a day and I really didn't feel like explaining to a stranger how Anya's parents had been killed and her hand crushed in a road accident.' Raina turned the sides of her mouth down, and Alistair saw hurt in her eyes.

'So Anya stuck up for you. Good girl.'

'Yes, she did. The woman just laughed and I said, "You heard." She made herself scarce then.'

'I hope she felt ashamed of herself.' Alistair wished he'd been there to defend them both.

'Probably not. I expect she's got a story that

she tells everyone about a horrible woman who encourages her child to be rude...' Raina broke off as Anya started to tug at her hand. 'What is it, sweetie?'

'Can we have some ice cream, Mum?' Anya had spotted a sign outside the lakeside café.

Raina pretended to consider the request for a moment. 'Okay. That sounds like a good idea.'

If there was nothing he could do about the everyday cruelty of the world, then at least he could buy the ice cream. 'I'll get it. Would you like to come and help choose, Anya?'

Anya nodded, slipping her hand into his, and he started to make for the café before Raina got a chance to pull her purse out of her bag.

Having Alistair along made all the difference. Raina didn't have to juggle with bags and keeping hold of Anya's hand, and he seemed genuinely to love playing with Anya. He made her a paper boat to float on the lake, and spun the duck food pellets so that they landed right in front of whichever duck Anya pointed out to him. He wiped melted ice cream from her hand and carried her when she got tired. And he talked to her about everything they saw, his own interest in the things around them matching that of an inquisitive three-year-old.

All that was left for Raina to do was to watch and enjoy. And to try not to think about how things might have been. Alistair was here with one purpose in mind, and if it didn't seem like that to Anya, then Raina should remember it.

After they'd explored the park, Alistair took them for afternoon tea in a smart hotel. As he ushered them into the plush reception area, Raina wondered if this wasn't a little too much for Anya, but Alistair held her hand, pointing out the twinkling chandeliers to her, and she was entranced.

'These are the stairs that all the princesses use.' He stopped at the bottom of a wide, sweeping staircase, and Anya nodded gravely.

'Uncle Alistair…' She held up her arms and Alistair picked her up so that she could see the twinkling lights that cascaded down the stairwell. Raina saw Anya's head bob back and forth, taking in everything around her, as he walked slowly up the centre of the red stair carpet.

The tea table was set with fine china cups and saucers, and heavy silver cutlery, on a snowy white tablecloth. A smiling waitress brought a high chair for Anya and Alistair pulled a chair back for Raina.

'This is really nice...' Raina sat down, feeling a little like an imposter. This looked a lot like a handsome man bringing his wife and daughter for afternoon tea. Alistair's attentiveness certainly bore that conclusion out, if anyone was tempted to jump to it.

He nodded. 'What do you think, Anya? Do you like it?'

'Yes. I like the pretty cups.'

'They're really nice, aren't they?' Alistair picked up a cup, keeping hold of it while Anya turned it in her hand, examining it. Everything he did was designed to get Anya to touch and manipulate things. 'Let's have a look at the menu, shall we?'

He started to read through the menu with Anya, and Raina picked hers up. This was way beyond what she could afford for afternoon tea. She nudged his foot with hers, under the table.

'Alistair, this is a bit pricey.' She whispered the words, wishing she'd thought to look at the menu on the reception desk.

'It's my treat...' He silenced her protests with

a firm look. 'Indulge me. Or I'll have to resort to unfair tactics and point out that Anya will be really disappointed if she doesn't get one of those cakes.'

He gestured towards the cake stands, which sat on a side table ready for serving. Anya looked round and her eyes suddenly became as round as saucers.

'Those *are* unfair tactics, Alistair.'

'What's a guy supposed to do? You have me outnumbered.' He grinned and Raina's heart melted.

'This is a lovely treat. Thank you.'

He caught the waitress's eye and ordered an afternoon tea for three. The young woman disappeared and then came back with cake stands containing small sandwiches and cakes, and a pot of tea. There was also a beaker of orange juice for Anya, and a glass of champagne for Raina.

'Alistair!'

'Come on. I know you like it.' He filled his own glass from the bottle of sparkling water that the waitress had brought.

'And this is part of your strategy, is it? Making the mothers tipsy while you spoil their children.' Raina selected a couple of sandwiches and put them onto a plate for Anya.

'One of my strategies. I'm just trying it out on you to see whether it works.' He grinned at her with such obvious relish that Raina smiled.

'It's working.' She couldn't help it. Alistair had made this into a fun day for both her and Anya.

He was enjoying this too. She could see it. Anya responded to his attention by being on her best behaviour, and Raina began to relax again. This *was* a very nice treat, and one that she couldn't afford these days.

It was nice to talk as well. Raina had forgotten how much she'd missed talking with Alistair about almost everything. This was the man she'd fallen in love with, the one who could make her laugh, and had something interesting to say on just about every subject under the sun...

'Mummy...' Anya suddenly started to rock in her chair, as if she wanted to get down from the table. Then she slid her residual limb into the front of her cardigan and Raina's heart fell. Not now. Please not now, when they were having such a nice time.

Alistair was looking round, at a pair of middle-aged women, who had arrived at the table next to theirs. Both were staring at Anya, and one had actually turned in her seat to do so.

Alistair grinned at them broadly and they both looked away. Raina gave Anya a smile and tried to get her interested in choosing a cake.

It seemed that the women weren't going to give up, though. They started to talk, glancing every now and then in Anya's direction, and Raina caught some of the words.

'She should cover that arm up. It's not very nice...'

She felt herself flush, and saw Alistair's face darken. Now, of all times, he'd heard what was going on behind his back.

'I just can't work up an appetite, you know... People should be more considerate.'

Alistair turned in his seat suddenly and Raina winced. The women had turned their gazes back onto Anya, looking as if they were both sucking lemons.

'Hi. My name's Alistair Duvall.' He took his wallet from his pocket, producing his card and reaching over to put it on the women's table. 'I'm a director of a charity that produces prosthetic limbs for kids, like my niece here. You seem interested, and I'm always on the lookout for volunteers to help with our work.'

One of the women looked away, and the other shot him an outraged glare. Alistair gave her his most easygoing smile. 'We're very flexible over hours…'

'The cheek of it!' The woman glared at Alistair and got up from the table, walking over to the waitress, her companion picking up her handbag and following. Alistair winked at Anya and she gave him an effusive smile, clearly understanding that he'd scored a victory on her behalf.

The women were talking to the waitress and pointing to a table by the window. The waitress shook her head, and the women walked over to it anyway. The debate seemed about to get heated, and the waitress indicated the *Reserved* sign, displayed prominently at the centre of the table. The women tossed their heads and left, and the waitress came hurrying over.

'I'm so terribly sorry. I heard what those

women said, and it's beyond unacceptable. Would you like me to call the manager?'

'Yes…'

'No.' Raina silenced Alistair with a glare. 'Thank you, we really appreciate your concern. But I think it's best if we let it drop now.'

'As you wish. I would have done anything I could to prevent this…' The waitress was clearly upset about what she'd heard. 'Please let me know if there's anything else you need. Some more tea, perhaps?'

'That would be very nice. And thank you for your kindness.' Alistair gave her an incandescent smile and the waitress grinned back, hurrying away.

He reached for the cake stand so that Anya could choose which cake she wanted, and put the small cupcake decorated with pink icing and sugar pearls onto her plate for her. Raina knew how he felt, though. The same outrage that she felt when people treated her daughter as if she had no feelings at all had been written all over his face.

And he'd called Anya his niece. He had to call her something, she supposed, and Anya had started to call him *Uncle* the way she did all grown-ups that she liked. If they'd still been married, Anya really would have been his niece.

Raina couldn't think about that. She picked up the teapot and poured the tea. The best thing she could do for Alistair now was to show him that the incident hadn't spoiled their day.

CHAPTER SEVEN

ALISTAIR LEANED BACK on the sofa, closing his eyes. 'I never realised that they were so exhausting.'

Raina laughed. 'You have higher standards than I do. I can't keep your level of play intensity up for that long.'

Alistair had thrown himself into his task for the day like a bull at a gate. After they'd returned home, every moment had been spent with Anya, playing with her and finding things to delight her. When she'd brought Anya back downstairs in her pyjamas for a bedtime story, she'd fallen asleep after the first page.

'It's harder than I thought. I've heard about people staring but you don't really get the full force of it until you experience it. I just can't imagine how anyone could be so downright nasty as those women were.'

'You don't get many like that. And there are lots of people like that lovely waitress for everyone who's nasty.' Raina sat down in an arm-chair, stretching her limbs. 'Did you see her face when you asked her if she wanted to vol-unteer? I wasn't sure whether to laugh or beg you to stop.'

Alistair chuckled. 'Nothing like asking for volunteers. There are some people who'll vol-unteer for anything, and others who run a mile.'

'What would you have done if she'd said she *had* volunteered?'

'There wasn't any danger of that. Trust me.'

It was nice having someone to talk to in the quiet evening hours. Someone to share her day with. Raina had missed that, and she'd missed Alistair.

'You've had a hard time of it these last few years.' His thought came out of nowhere, in the way that evening thoughts often did.

'I guess… I had to get through it. For Anya's sake.'

'You had your own grief to contend with…' The open-ended statement was an invitation for her to talk.

'It was hard to think about that. My mum and dad were both devastated. Dad couldn't even go to Anya's beside at the hospital without breaking down. And Mum sat with me at her side until she almost collapsed with exhaustion. She didn't sleep for thirty-six hours.'

'And you?' His face seemed soft in the shadows.

'I made up my mind that I had to be the one who coped. I gave Mum a timetable, and made her go home to eat and go to bed, even though she couldn't sleep. I kept Dad up to date with what was happening with Anya and gradually he managed to be with her again. They worked through their grief and...they found a way to care for Anya again, without constantly thinking of Andrew.'

'And now?'

'They love her to bits. They always have, they just needed a bit of time to readjust. But they're the best, they're always there for me and they'll take Anya without question if I have to go and do something. They help me out if I need something for Anya and I can't afford it.'

He nodded. 'So when did *you* grieve?'

It was a question that Raina didn't know

quite how to answer. 'I...don't know. Somewhere in between settling Andrew and Theresa's estate and working through the adoption process for Anya.'

'And *did* you speak with anyone about it?'

He'd asked the question before and she'd shut him down. This time Raina couldn't. 'No, not really. If I'd spoken about it, it would all have seemed too much to bear. Keeping it all to myself kept me strong.'

'That's not the Raina I used to know.' Alistair was looking at her thoughtfully.

'Life has a habit of changing us.'

Maybe he saw the same thing that had just become clear to Raina. That she understood his silence a little better, because it was what she'd just admitted to doing herself. She'd bottled up her own grief because she'd had to help her parents and Anya.

And she still hadn't told him everything. The grief at finding she couldn't have more children was hers alone. Alistair was an honourable man, and if she'd told him about that while they were still married he would have felt duty bound to stop the divorce and try again. But there had been nothing left any more to try for.

Everyone had their secrets. Those few things that they never discussed. The more she thought about it, the more her own actions seemed similar to the ones she'd condemned Alistair for.

'Did you ever take some time for yourself?'

'The first anniversary hit everyone hard, but afterwards things started to get a little better. Then my own grief hit me and I cried for a long time. Every night, for months. Then I could move forward.'

Alistair said nothing for a long time, seeming deep in thought. 'I guess…we all need to feel our losses. However painful it is, it helps us move forward.'

That seemed to be all he was willing to venture on the subject. But another chunk of the barrier between them had crumbled away. And the Alistair that she was beginning to see wasn't so very different from the person she saw when she looked in the mirror.

'Would you like me to make some tea?' He spoke again.

An echo of the past. One where they'd get back home, both exhausted from their day's work, and fall onto the sofa together. Alistair would make her tea and they'd go to bed, curling up in each other's arms to sleep.

'Yes, thanks. Tea would be nice.'

Raina had shown him up to the small spare bedroom, apologising that it was a bit cramped and hoping he'd be comfortable. Right now, all he wanted to do was to lie down and let the day slip away in sleep.

She was braver than even he had thought she might be. When they'd divorced, all their assets had been divided up in a simple fifty-fifty split. It had been enough for Alistair to put a deposit down on a house and start again. Their salaries had been much the same, both young doctors working hard to build their careers. He'd imagined that Raina would have had the ability buy a place much the same as his.

And now he felt guilty. Raina's small cottage felt like a palace, but that was because it was full of her own little touches. Pictures on the mantelpiece. Candles in the hearth and warm colours for cushions and curtains. Anya's toys, and Raina's books. The tiny garden was full of flowers, with plants to attract butterflies and bees, and a bird table. But she didn't have the room that Alistair's house provided him with, and it was clear that she'd done most of the decoration herself.

She'd made the decision that he had struggled with. When she'd told him that she was pregnant, he'd worried about how he was going to support her and the baby. His only thought had been how he could keep up with the mortgage and afford to give his wife and child everything. But Raina had taken a different approach. She'd given up work and downsized, counting her pennies and spending them wisely. She'd embraced the life that he'd dreaded and had made a home that was filled with love.

And that home didn't include him. He could take a look at her life, like a child staring through the window of a toyshop, but he couldn't be a part of it any more. Alistair turned over restlessly in bed. If he couldn't give her everything any more, then he could still give her and Anya something.

He slept well and woke early, waiting in bed until he'd heard that Raina and Anya had finished in the bathroom. Then he showered and went downstairs. Anya looked at him wide-eyed, clearly not expecting to see him.

'You see, I told you that you'd have Uncle Alistair to play with today…' Raina shot him a smile. 'How did you sleep? I hope we didn't wake you.'

'No…' Alistair sat down at the kitchen table, greeting Anya, and Raina put a cup of coffee down in front of him. 'Why were you up in the night?'

Anya had a nightmare. She mouthed the words over her daughter's head.

'There was a monster.' Anya turned to him, her dark eyes serious.

'And what happened? He can't have eaten you, because you're right here,' Alistair replied.

'I shouted and shouted. And Mummy came and bashed him.'

'It was just a shadow on the curtain, sweetie.' Raina laughed, sitting down at the table.

Anya turned to him, stretching over to whisper in his ear, 'It was a real monster. Mummy frightened him and he jumped out of the window.'

'I'm sure she did. Mummy's terribly brave.

And pretty frightening when she wants to be.'
He heard Raina's snort of laughter.

'Yes, she is.'

'Good thing she's on our side, eh?'

Anya considered the question carefully. 'Yes.
It's a good thing.'

How on earth had he not heard the commotion? Perhaps he had and didn't remember getting up, but Alistair was pretty sure he'd slept like a baby. Monster-free, all night.

Then he realised. If he slept on his right side, then he was to all intents and purposes completely deaf, his hearing aid on the bedside cabinet and his good ear buried in the pillow. And he'd woken on his right side this morning...

So much for the newfound feeling that maybe he could have risen to the challenge that Raina had. He couldn't even be there to fend off shadows on the curtains and help calm Anya's fears.

'Toast?' Raina's voice came to his rescue.
'Or would you prefer cereal?'

'Toast, thank you.' He grinned up at her as she reached into one of the kitchen cabinets and put a jar of peanut butter on the table. She'd remembered... 'I haven't had peanut butter and toast in ages.'

'You'll need a good breakfast. You never know when you're going to find yourself on monster duty.'

'I'll give it a go. If they look too scary I might just have to call you in.' He smiled at Anya. 'Your mum's the best monster-fighter I know.'

Anya nodded. She knew that already. And Alistair knew already that, try as he may, he'd never make the kind of parent that Raina did.

Raina had done the washing up and then found herself at a loose end. Alistair was absorbed once more in the business of playing with Anya, and it appeared that she could take the day off. But she couldn't think of anything she wanted to do more than watch him.

Anya had shown him the garden, the things they'd planted together, and the tree where the fairies lived. The butterfly bush, and the bird table. He'd played football with her on the grass, and Anya had copied his victory dance when she'd managed to get the ball past him and score a goal. Raina sipped her tea, relaxing in the sunshine. It all looked exhausting.

And he seemed to be getting somewhere. The games all led to one moment. The one where he sat with her on the sitting-room floor, passing a small squishy ball from one hand to the other and gently dropping it into Anya's lap. The two of them talked for a while, and then Alistair reached for the box that had lain unnoticed on the floor next to the sofa.

He took out the prosthetic, talking to her all the time. Anya shook her head and he put it down on the floor, out of sight. They batted the ball back and forth between them and he tried again. This time Anya picked up the prosthetic, using it as a scoop to send the ball flying back in his direction. Alistair retrieved it and sat down with her again.

He was so patient. So kind. Raina held her breath as he rolled the soft fabric liner onto her arm, and carefully fitted the prosthetic over it, activating the suction pad. Then he took the ball and held it out to her.

She didn't know what to do. Anya had managed with one hand so long that she didn't understand that she could throw the ball better using two. Alistair gently helped her, curling his hands around her arms, showing her how to pick the ball up.

'That's really good, Anya. Shall we show

Mummy?' He looked up at her and Raina wiped away the tears that had formed in her eyes.

'What have you got to show me?' Raina got up out of her chair and sat down cross-legged on the floor.

Alistair helped Anya to pick the ball up and roll it across the floor. Raina retrieved it and rolled it back and Anya reached for it with one hand. Alistair guided her other arm forward, and she picked the ball up.

Raina could only watch, her throat blocked with emotion. Alistair stepped in with a little encouragement. 'Nice one, Anya. Let's see if we can score a goal, shall we?'

Her first try landed right in Raina's lap, so there was no opportunity to let the ball past her. Alistair gave an exaggerated groan of disappointment. 'Well done. We'll get her the next time.'

Raina rolled the ball back and Anya threw it again. This time it shot past her and bounced against the wall.

'Way to go! Victory dance?' Alistair got to his feet. Together he and Anya did their victory dance, and Raina laughed, clapping her hands together.

* * *

Anya had used the arm for about an hour and then Alistair had decided she'd had enough. After lunch, another session with building bricks, when Anya had unexpectedly used the prosthetic arm to support herself as she climbed to her feet.

'I don't know how to thank you.' Raina stood with him in the doorway, wishing he didn't have to go.

'I've had a great time. I should be thanking you.' He slung his weekend bag over his shoulder. 'You'll try her again with it tomorrow?'

'Yes. I hope I can get her to wear it.' This meant so much to Raina. She wasn't sure that she'd be able to be as patient and relaxed about it as Alistair had been.

'Just offer it to her and if she doesn't want it then put it to one side. You'll bring her in on Tuesday?'

'Yes, what time?'

'I thought lunchtime. I'll take you both to lunch and then we can go somewhere.'

'Haven't you got work to catch up on?' Raina dismissed the thrill that the idea of spending a whole afternoon with Alistair provoked. 'You know…all the things you haven't done this weekend.'

'That can wait. I think it's important that we keep up the momentum and consolidate the progress we've made.' He smiled, mischief dancing in his tawny eyes. 'And I had such a great time this weekend.'

'I did too. Let me bring some lunch.' Raina couldn't afford to take him out for an afternoon tea, but she could make something nice. 'Then perhaps we could go to the Science Museum?'

He chuckled. 'Is this an outing for me or for Anya?'

'She'll like it too.'

'In that case, it's a deal. I can't wait.'

He turned to go, and Raina reached out, touching his arm. Before she could stop herself, or think about the consequences, she'd stood on her toes and kissed his cheek. 'Thank you, for all you've done for Anya.'

The look in his eyes wouldn't let her free. As Raina brushed her lips against his, she felt him shiver.

'What's that one for?'

If she told him, she wouldn't be able to go back. If he knew just how much she wanted him right now, maybe he wouldn't be able to go back either.

'That one's just from me.'

He nodded, his fingers brushing his lips, right where she'd kissed him. 'Then I'll treasure it.'

Alistair turned and walked to his car. Raina watched him go, waving as the car drew away. The house seemed so quiet now without him. She tiptoed upstairs and into Anya's room, leaning over to kiss her forehead.

Before Anya had gone to bed, Alistair had checked thoroughly and proclaimed the room entirely monster-free. Maybe if Anya woke, she'd think of him and be reassured. And if Raina managed to sleep at all, maybe she'd dream of him.

Raina sat on the park bench, sunshine filtering through the trees that surrounded the small square outside The Watchlight Trust's offices. Anya was running around the small square of grass, letting off steam after a play session with Kaia, and Alistair had gone to fetch coffee.

It had become an afternoon ritual. The high railings around the square meant that it was safe for Anya to run around if Raina kept her eye on her, and she and Alistair could get some fresh air and talk.

He sauntered towards her, two cups of coffee in his hands. So like it had once been… Raina dismissed the thought and accepted the coffee with a smile.

'So… How's it all going with Kaia?' He sat down on the bench next to her.

'Really well. She has a nice way with Anya, and she loves working with children. Her understanding of the way the prosthetics are made means that she's able to be very responsive to Anya's needs.'

Alistair nodded. 'Yeah, she's doing well. I'm thinking of asking her to head up the technical side of the project team. Ben's expressed an interest in moving on to something different in a few weeks' time, when we've got the finishing touches to the prosthetic designs sorted out.'

'That sounds like a good idea. For both of them. Kaia's interested in seeing the project through, and Ben's always got something new in his sights.' Raina had come to respect the way Alistair organised the charity's work teams, always listening to what each individual wanted and trying to develop their talents.

'And how about you? I'm keen to know if there's anything you think we could be doing better on this project.'

That was another way in which Alistair gained the respect of both his staff and his patients. He was always willing to listen, and Raina had realised how much it had hurt him when he was struggling to hear. Now that he was coping better with his deafness, he seemed more confident about his place in the world.

'I think…it's been a great experience, and I know that the other parents think so too. There is one thing, though.'

Alistair grinned. 'Okay. Fire away.'

'When we started out, I was pretty sure of what to expect. I knew the medical issues and it was really only the idea of what the Dream Team could and couldn't do that I had to get to grips with. But I know that some of the parents felt a little overwhelmed by it all.'

'They did?' Alistair's face clouded. 'Gabriel and I did our best to explain everything...'

'Yes, I know, and you did a great job. But some of them were coming to me to ask questions because they knew I'm a parent as well as a doctor. We ended up forming our own little support group.'

'Yes, I noticed that when all the parents were in the office together you all adjourned to the park for lunch. I thought that something of the sort was going on, and decided not to interfere. I reckoned you'd ask for my input if you needed it.'

Raina grinned. 'Yes. That's what I'm doing now. It worked well for us, because I'm a doctor and I understood a lot of the issues. But for other groups...'

Alistair nodded. 'So what are you saying? That we should make it official and form a patient support group for each intake of children? Wouldn't that undermine the whole point? It worked because it was an informal group.'

He hadn't taken the bait yet. Raina reckoned he would if she dangled it for long enough. 'I was just thinking that The Watchlight Trust could provide the facilities, a place to sit and maybe drinks, and that the group could use them to discuss whatever it wanted. Just a few sessions, maybe one a week, with a parent who's been through the process already.'

He nodded. 'It would be ideal if that parent happened to have the medical knowledge to answer questions as well. That kind of person's pretty hard to find.'

Raina resisted the temptation to tip the rest of her coffee into his lap. It was still lukewarm, and it might scald. 'Don't play hard to get with me, Alistair. It doesn't suit you.'

He chuckled. 'Oh, so you think easy suits me?'

It suited him a lot better than stand-offish and prickly. But, then, Raina hadn't been at her best when they'd started working together either. These last few weeks had seen a change in both of them.

'Easy is just fine.'

'Okay, then. It's been suggested to me that an informal family support group might be beneficial. I think it's a splendid idea and was wondering whether you'd be able to help us out with that. Since you're both a doctor and a parent.'

'Yes, I'd be happy to help.' Raina wrinkled her nose at him.

'That's great. Any ideas on how it might work?' He pulled a face back.

'Well, I could put some notes together for an introductory session. What to expect, and so on. We could take it from there maybe.'

'What do you think about involving one of the counsellors from the clinic?' Alistair had made sure that all the parents knew that they could use the counselling service that the clinic next door to the charity's offices ran.

'Yes, that would be a good idea. Maybe for just one of the sessions, so that the parents could get to know them and feel more confident about approaching you for counselling help if they needed it.'

'Right, then. Leave that side of it with me, and I'll organise it. And I'll leave the introductory session to you, shall I?' Alistair was clearly trying to keep the laughter from his voice, and failing miserably.

'Sounds good.'

They sat for a moment, watching Anya play in the sunshine. Alistair was grinning broadly now.

'So how did I do? Was I easy enough for you?'

'You did just fine. Ten out of ten...' Raina couldn't help laughing now, too.

She saw Anya bend down to examine something in the grass, and got to her feet to see what it was. The little girl decided to make a race of it back to where Alistair was sitting, but suddenly he was taking no notice of them. The pager on his belt was vibrating and Alistair twisted it round to look at the tiny screen and accept the message.

'Sorry, got to go. The clinic's paged me...' He was already on his feet, leaving his coffee on the bench behind him, and hurrying towards the entrance of the square.

It was like old times. But then they'd responded to the buzz of a pager together, and now she was left behind. Raina picked up his coffee, dumping it in the bin along with her own. Alistair had crossed the road and was taking the steps up to the front door of the clinic two at a time.

'Are we going back?' Anya was watching Alistair too, and Raina suddenly knew exactly what she was going to do next.

'Yes, sweetie. And we're going to run as fast as we can…' Raina collected her bag and took Anya's hand.

CHAPTER EIGHT

ONE OF THE nurses from the clinic met Alistair at the reception desk and before he had a chance to ask what the matter was, she had a reply for him.

'There's some trouble upstairs, in the group therapy room.'

Alistair nodded, making for the stairs. The clinic dealt with a number of PTSD patients and although the counsellors were skilled at nipping any disturbances in the bud, it was always a risk.

Upstairs, he found a group gathered around the door of one of the therapy rooms, the sound of yelling echoing out into the corridor. Everyone moved back as he approached, to clear his way to the door.

'Thanks, everyone. Shall we move it downstairs…?'

The group began to disperse and Alistair looked for Joe, the counsellor who would have been taking the group. He was nowhere in sight and he must be inside the room still, along with whoever it was that was shouting at the top of his voice. Then he saw Raina, hurrying along the corridor towards him.

'Where's Anya?' This was no situation for a child.

'I left her with Kaia. She let me through the connecting door to the clinic, and I followed the noise.'

A small tingle of excitement threaded through Alistair's veins. This was what it had been like when they'd first met. He'd been a newly minted doctor, while Raina had still been at medical school, and when she'd been rotated to his department the buzz of a pager in his pocket had meant just one thing. A shared glance, and they had been acting as one, hurrying to help. They'd moved past that first awkward meeting, on the banks of the Thames, when all Alistair had wanted Raina to do was stay out of the way and let him work.

'Okay. Listen out for me, will you?' There was no knowing what he might or might not be able to hear, but he knew for sure that if he missed something important, Raina would have his back.

She nodded, and he stepped in between her and the door, peering through the small pane of glass that gave a view of what was going on inside the room. It didn't look good and he was going to need Raina's help with this.

'The counsellor, Joe, is in there and it looks as if he's been hurt. Emma, one of the group, has stayed with him, she's able to help as she's a paramedic, but be aware that she has her own issues with confrontation. I don't know the guy who's doing all the shouting, he's a new patient. I'll try and calm him down, and if you can see an opportunity to get Joe and Emma out…'

He turned to Raina and she nodded. Alistair twisted the door handle quietly, opening the door.

Raina could hear the sound of a man's voice, full of rage and pain. As Alistair opened the door she could see inside. A man was pacing up and down, stopping only to strike his head with his hands.

Raina curled her fingers around Alistair's

arm, mouthing a warning. *Careful. That might not be PTSD.*

Alistair nodded in agreement. Whatever was happening here, there had obviously been a fight, because Joe was sitting in one of the easy chairs, a dark bruise forming on his cheek. He was clutching his shoulder, beads of perspiration on his brow as he tried to calm the pacing man. Next to him, Emma was supporting his arm across his body in the best position for a dislocated shoulder.

'Why don't you sit down, Stuart?' Joe's voice was strained but calm, as he tried to diffuse the situation.

'Can't.' Stuart struck his forehead with his hand, and turned suddenly, closing on Joe with his fists clenched. Emma flung herself between them and Joe tried to push her to one side, wincing in pain as he did so.

But Alistair was there. In between the two men, firmly but gently crowding Stuart back, channelling his attention away from Joe. Putting himself in the firing line would allow Raina to get Joe and Emma out of the room. Raina hurried towards them.

'Emma? Are you okay?' She whispered the

words and Emma nodded. Raina had already seen the scars on her neck and that three fingers from one hand were missing, but Emma had clearly chosen to forget that she was a patient here, and her training as a paramedic was giving her the courage to face this situation.

'What do you think?' Raina had a good idea of what was wrong with Joe's shoulder, but she wanted Emma to stay involved.

'Looks like a dislocated shoulder,' Emma replied, and Raina bent down, running her fingers over it.

'I think you're right.' Raina turned to Joe. He was obviously in a lot of pain but he seemed to be holding himself together. 'Do you think you can walk?'

'Yes. I can walk.'

The smack of flesh hitting flesh reached Raina's ears and she turned to see Alistair's head snap back.

'Not again!' He muttered the words. That was the eye that had been infected and the blow seemed to have fallen pretty much in the same place as the cut had been. 'Stuart, there's no need for that, mate.'

Stuart seemed to calm once more, and Raina

turned her attention back to Joe. Emma helped her to get him to his feet, and supported him towards the door, while Raina positioned herself between them and Stuart, in case he should break free from Alistair.

'Is Alistair going to be all right?' As soon as the door was closed behind them, Emma turned to her.

'He seems to have everything under control.' Raina hoped he did. She wanted to go back and make sure, but that wasn't where she was needed at the moment. Ushering Joe away from the door and towards one of the consulting rooms was the last thing that Raina wanted, but she knew that Alistair was relying on her to do it.

As they made their way slowly along the corridor, a couple of male nurses came hurrying past them. Raina breathed a sigh of relief. If Alistair couldn't calm Stuart and he became violent, that would even the odds considerably.

She and Emma got Joe onto the consulting-room couch, and Raina busied herself, examining Joe's shoulder carefully. It looked like an anterior dislocation, and she called down to the nurses' station, asking for an X-ray.

'That was a brave thing to do, Emma.' Joe spoke to her softly.

Emma shrugged, but she seemed pleased. 'It's all part of the job, Joe. And at least Stuart didn't have a machete on him.'

So that was the cause of Emma's scars. Raina shivered at the thought. But Emma didn't need her sympathy at the moment, she needed to know that she could still do her job. Raina had to balance that with her concern for Emma's welfare, as well as Joe's.

'Is your wrist okay, Emma?' Raina nodded towards the light support that Emma wore on her arm, as she tucked a pillow against Joe's arm to make him more comfortable while they waited for the X-ray technician to arrive.

'Yeah, it's fine. I broke it four months ago and it still aches a bit sometimes, so I use the support.'

'How did you do that?' Raina asked the question casually, tending to Joe as she did so. Emma's scars were obviously more than four months old.

'Stupidity mainly. I tripped over a box of envelopes in the conference room. Gabriel needed his very best bedside manner as I cried like a baby.'

For all her bravery, Emma's hand was shaking. It couldn't have been easy for her to relive the experience of an attack.

Joe puffed out a breath. 'Trust me, Emma, I'm thinking of doing the same.' He was clearly concerned for Emma too, but his arm must hurt a great deal.

'When we have the X-ray we'll be able to make you more comfortable, Joe,' Raina reassured him, and Emma nodded in agreement. Concentrating on Joe seemed to steady her.

'Thanks.' Joe nodded. 'Where's Alistair?'

'I'm not sure. I'll find out when the X-ray technician gets here, and if he's available I'll get him to review the X-rays and do the reduction if that's what you'd like.' He was a member of staff at the clinic, and he specialised in traumatic limb injury. And Joe knew Alistair and must trust him.

'Yeah. Thanks.'

'All right. Let's all take a breath, shall we? Not too big a breath, Joe, I need you to stay still if you can.' Raina filled her lungs, puffing out the tension, and Emma followed suit, grinning.

The X-ray technician arrived, and Emma followed them down to the X-ray suite. As Joe was wheeled into the radiography room, Alistair caught up with them.

'Everything okay?'

Raina nodded, flashing a glance in Emma's direction, and Alistair took the hint.

'Cup of tea, Emma? You've done your bit now. You can leave Joe to us.'

Emma nodded. 'I could do with one.'

Alistair shepherded Emma away, smiling and talking with her as they went. Raina sat down with a bump, expecting that he might be a while, but he returned after just a couple of minutes.

'Is Emma okay?'

Alistair nodded. 'One of the other counsellors is sitting with her in the coffee lounge. She's a bit shaky, but this has been a huge step forward for her. How's Joe?'

'Probable anterior dislocation of the shoulder, the X-rays should confirm it and whether there are any fractures. What about Stuart?'

'He's much calmer, now, and there are a couple of nurses with him. It looks as if this is some underlying psychiatric condition. He's a new patient, and when he went through the screening process there was no warning of this. His wife's on her way and we'll decide what to do when she gets here.'

Raina nodded. 'Are you going to let me look at that eye this time?'

Alistair grinned. 'I thought you'd never ask.'

He sat down, and Raina carefully examined the eye. Standing between his outstretched legs, their physical closeness made it hard to keep her mind on the job. Hard not to think about how different things were between them now.

'Okay, there's no damage been done to your eye, just the soft tissue around it. A couple of weeks and you'll have your flawless good looks back.' Raina turned away smiling, as if the part about the flawless good looks was a joke. It was far from that.

'Well, that's good to know.' Alistair snorted with laughter, looking up as Joe was wheeled back out of the radiography room. 'Hey, there, Joe. How are you doing?'

'Not so bad.' Joe's face was ashen with pain now.

'Joe would like you to look at the X-rays, Alistair, and take over his treatment.' It was natural that Joe would want that, but it still hurt a little. Being a mum was the thing that fulfilled Raina, but she still missed being a doctor.

'Thanks, Alistair. Only the best…' Joe murmured the words and Alistair raised his eyebrows.

'I'm only the best when Raina's not in the room.' The look in his eyes told Raina that this wasn't an empty compliment, he really meant it. And that suddenly made everything all right.

Alistair had reviewed the X-rays, and he and Raina had agreed on a course of treatment. It was Joe's prerogative to choose who he wanted as his doctor, but Alistair's to choose who to work with, and Raina *was* the best. They carried out the gentle manipulation of Joe's arm back into the shoulder joint, working together as if the last five years had never happened.

But it had. When Joe's arm had been immobilised in a sling, and he'd been put into the charge of one of the nurses, the distance between them seemed to grow again.

And then Raina crossed the divide. Running the cold-water tap in the basin in the corner of the consulting room, she soaked a flannel and motioned for him to sit down.

'Ah. That feels better. Thanks.' His eye was beginning to throb and the cold, moist flannel felt good. It felt good to have Raina there too, holding the flannel gently against his face, her fingers cool and comforting.

'I'm going to have to go in a minute. I should take Anya home.'

'Yeah. I should catch up with Emma.' But Raina was here now. Just a few more moments before they left the fantasy behind and went back to reality. That what they'd once been to each other was in the past now, and couldn't be re-created.

Raina rinsed the flannel under the cold-water tap and reapplied it to his face. It was all Alistair could do not to sigh.

'She was so brave. Staying with Joe like that after what happened to her.'

'Yeah. You know, the more I work here the less I feel I know. And the more I feel our patients have to teach me.' Emma had come to terms with her past in a way that Alistair doubted he ever could.

'I think that shows you're doing things right, doesn't it? Close your eye for a moment.'

It hurt to close just one eye, so Alistair closed both. He heard the sound of water running and then felt Raina's cool fingers and the flannel on his face. If this wasn't the time to say what he'd been feeling for the last week, then that time was never going to come.

'Anya's a case in point. She has no thought of being disadvantaged, she just knows that she's a little different and compensates. I think I should follow her example.'

The flannel moved, and he felt Raina's finger, tapping gently against the side of his face in a sign that he could open his eyes now.

'She's only three. I don't want her to ever feel that she's disadvantaged, but I have to accept that the time might come when the world tells her differently.'

'Maybe. But if she keeps listening to her mother, she can't go far wrong.'

Raina raised her eyebrows. 'That wouldn't be an admission that I'm always right, would it?'

'Nah. I've got enough to do at the moment, I wouldn't want to add you to my list, after you've fainted from shock.'

'Wise move.' Raina laughed, rinsing the flannel in the sink and hanging it over the tap. 'I think you're good to go now.'

He was good to go. A little wiser for the time he'd spent with Raina, but that was never going to be a reason for them to be together again. He might understand the reasons for their divorce a little better, but that just meant that he knew that there was no going back.

Alistair got to his feet. 'I'll see you later in the week?'

'Yes, I've arranged for a session with Kaia on Thursday.' She paused, as if she'd just thought of something. 'Were you serious when you said I could run with the parent support idea?'

'Yes, of course. If you want to, that is.'

Raina nodded. 'Yes, I want to. Thanks.'

CHAPTER NINE

RAINA UNPACKED HER weekend bag for the third time. She didn't usually have this amount of trouble deciding what to wear.

'I like this one, Mummy...' Anya was sitting on the bed, sorting through the rejects pile, and held up a filmy, see-through blouse. She was using her prosthetic hand much more now, and as well as being able to use it to manipulate things better, the droop of her left shoulder as she struggled to equalise the length of both limbs had been corrected.

'No, not that one, sweetie.' Not for a conference. Certainly not for a conference with Alistair.

And this was important. The Watchlight Trust had been working on this for months and the list of attendees had been carefully selected.

Not to mention the venue. Raina wasn't going to even think about the venue.

'What about a suit?' Raina held the dark grey skirt and jacket up against herself.

Anya wrinkled her nose and shook her head. Maybe she was right. Raina had bought the suit years ago, when she and Alistair had been divorcing. She hadn't worn it much, the colour was too drab.

'A dress, then?' She had a few nice dresses that she could team with a jacket to smarten them up.

Anya nodded, throwing herself over onto her stomach. She was bored with this now, and if Anya was bored with a dressing-up session then it had definitely gone on too long.

'Okay, the dress it is. And this one…' Raina put the two dresses aside, along with a jacket that matched both, and surveyed the rumpled pile of clothes on the bed. Now for the cocktail party…

That was the most difficult. Raina had three suitable dresses, all of which had been bought while she'd been married to Alistair. Each one of them held memories.

Anya started to sing, and Raina joined in. Somehow that seemed to lessen the tension. Her little girl needed two hands to throw clothes around on the bed with, or make what-ever mess she wanted. *This* was why she was doing this, nothing else.

'All right. Last one, Anya. Blue or black?' She held the two dresses up.

'Red!'

Anya loved that dress. So did Raina. And so had Alistair...

'You're sure?'

'Yes, Mummy. It's beautiful.' Anya rolled off the bed, taking a pile of blouses with her, and walked over to the wardrobe, tugging at the skirt of the red dress.

Raina took the dress from the wardrobe. She had to wear something, and she always felt comfortable in this dress. She bent down and kissed her daughter.

'I'll wear it for you, then.' Not Alistair. 'It'll remind me how much I'm going to miss you when I'm away.'

'It's only two days. And we're going to the zoo. Grandad promised.'

From the number of things that her father had promised Anya they'd do, it was clear that her daughter would prefer it to be three days. Even though her father had barely been able to look at Anya after the accident, he doted on the little girl now.

'He did. And you know that Grandad never breaks a promise if he can help it.'

'He would turn into a donkey if he did.' Anya cackled with laughter, clearly quite liking the idea.

'Or a wiggly worm.' Raina wiggled her finger and Anya nodded sagely. 'Are you going to help me clear all this up?'

'Yes. Make it all tidy.' Anya liked tidying up even more than she liked making a mess. Her mother had told her that she was like Andrew in that, and that when he and Raina had been little, it had always been Raina who'd scattered her toys around and Andrew who'd put them neatly back in place. Anya's idea of order wasn't always entirely practical, but that was okay.

'Shall we see if we can make a rainbow?' Anya's dresses were arranged in rainbow order in her wardrobe, and Raina's mother had even made her a little orange dress to fill the gap.

'Yes…'

'All right, then. What comes first?' Raina picked up the suit, wondering where grey might fit in. Somewhere in the corner, probably where it couldn't be seen.

'Red!' Anya picked up a red blouse from the pile on the floor, brandishing it. Raina laughed, and suddenly the conference seemed less menacing.

DeMarco Pharmaceuticals' conference centre was based in Sussex. The address suggested an ancient building, set in sleepy countryside, but nothing could be further from the truth. Gabriel's father had offered his company's state-of-the-art centre for The Watchlight Trust's conference.

The building was mostly hidden from the road by trees, which fell away to reveal a structure that shimmered in the sunshine. Curved glass and steel seemed to rise organically from a large lake to one side. This would be tomorrow's treasured landmark, a tribute to the twenty-first century.

The glass-sided reception area was triple height and flooded with light, the sound from a glass waterfall wall plashing quietly in the background. After the heat of the road it was cool and soothing, but Raina felt her cheeks redden when she saw Alistair.

He was dressed in a dark blue open-necked shirt and trousers. Just the right combination of crisp and casual. And mouthwateringly sexy. Maybe that part was just because Raina knew exactly what was beneath the shirt. How many times had she traced the ridges of his chest with her fingers?

'You made it, then?' He left Heidi talking to the receptionist, and approached Raina. 'What do you think?'

'It's…stunning. Not exactly the kind of place you'd expect a charity to be using.'

Alistair chuckled. 'Yes. We made it clear on the invitation that the place is lent to us free of charge by DeMarco Pharmaceuticals. I wouldn't want anyone to think we have this kind of money to throw around. Let me give you the guided tour…'

'Aren't you busy?' He could just show her to her room and let her explore for herself if he wanted. The kind of breath-catching awe that this place promised might be best to ex-perience without the additional excitement of Alistair at her side.

'No, Heidi's making sure that everything goes smoothly, as usual. Gabriel's on his way down with the Dream Team and I'm at a loose end until the delegates start to arrive in a couple of hours.'

Alistair bent to pick up her case, the twitch at the corner of his mouth indicating that he'd noticed its size and weight. 'Maybe we'll drop this off first.'

'Yes. I…um…wasn't sure what to wear so I ended up packing for every eventuality.' Every eventuality apart from this. She hadn't brought a blindfold, which was about the only thing that could stop her from noticing him. Or a peg for her nose, so that his clean scent couldn't pleasure her senses.

'Evidently.' He strolled over to the reception desk and Heidi handed him a key. It seemed that Alistair was intent on playing porter, and she followed him through to the back of the reception area and into a glass-sided corridor.

She could now see that the building was crescent shaped, curved around a seating area with gardens and flowing water. The slate paving stones were broken up by twisting lines of thick glass, and when Raina looked carefully she could see running water beneath. The overall effect was one of peace and calm, as the man-made structure embraced the natural world outside.

The guest rooms were on the far side of the building, at the tips of the crescent. Cool and calm, with pale wood furniture and large windows, shaded by trees for privacy. Alistair placed her suitcase next to the bed, and gave her the key.

'I hope you'll be comfortable.'

Physical comfort was hardly in doubt. When she sat down on the cream quilted counterpane, the large bed was just the right mixture of springy and soft. And Raina imagined that the sunlight filtering through the trees in the morning would make this a lovely room to wake up in. If she tossed and turned at night, that would be a matter of mental discomfort.

And the best way to get over that was to face the situation head on. Inure herself to Alistair and their surroundings. Wear herself out so that she couldn't help sleeping tonight.

'I'm sure I shall. Does your offer to show

me around still stand?' She gave him a bright smile.

'Yes, of course.'

Alistair had always liked this place. It did exactly what it was meant to do, helping delegates relax and focus. Right now he felt anything but relaxed, and completely focussed on Raina.

Beautiful wasn't exactly the word. It intimated a calculation that had never entered Raina's head. She was a force of nature, drawn to colour and texture because that was what she loved, without any notion of looking good in it. But she did. Her pale linen jacket, blue trousers and patterned top would have been a nice outfit on their own. Combined with Raina's dark hair, her long legs and the graceful way that she moved, the effect was nothing short of stunning.

'There are enough solar panels on the roof to provide power, even in the winter.' Alistair concentrated on his role as tour guide. 'Food is sourced from local farmers where possible, and the woodlands over to the left are being maintained to encourage wildlife and rare species of plants.'

'So it's not as high-tech as it looks.' She smiled up at him.

'Oh, it's high-tech all right. Wait until you get into the shower. But the technology is all about making as little impact on the environment as possible, and nurturing the things we want to save for future generations.'

'For Anya.' As usual, Raina managed to bring a lofty idea right back down to the personal.

'Yep.' As far as the new generation was concerned, Alistair was happy to keep it a lofty idea. Thinking too much about how he felt about the personal was a road he shouldn't take with Raina.

They wandered through the large, open-plan spaces, filled with smaller-scale seating areas to encourage people to circulate and form groups. The lecture theatres, and the restaurant, the folding doors opening out onto the paved garden that was at the heart of the building. She commented on the underfloor streams, walking along one as if it were a tightrope, one foot in front of the other. So many people took this building the wrong way. It was supposed to be enjoyed, with the same child-like pleasure that Raina showed.

'How does all this sound to you?' As they walked past a sheet of water flowing over contoured stone, she turned to him suddenly.

'Um… A bit crackly.' Alistair didn't put his hearing aid in until after he'd washed and shaved in the morning. With it, the water in the basin sounded as if it could be heard half-way down the street. No one else had considered that a place surrounded by water might be a little unnerving.

'But if you look at it, it helps normalise the sound?'

'Yes, it does. I've been using that technique and it helps.' Maybe if he stared at Raina for long enough he might normalise the way he felt about her, but Alistair doubted it.

'So…this conference. It's a big challenge for you. Groups of people all talking at once.'

She would help him if he asked. It was one thing to have her soothe a blackened eye, though, and quite another to start relying on her to help him with his more permanent needs. 'I can adjust my hearing aid. Hopefully that's all under control.'

He turned away from the water and the rushing sound subsided. 'It's half an hour before the delegates' check-in opens and I'm back on duty. Would you like some coffee?' He gestured towards the drinks counter, which was already open and being stocked with supplies.

'Yes, thank you. It would be nice to sit here for a while. You can tell me a little more about what to expect over the next few days.' She retreated to the exact place in the garden where the activity in the restaurant and the sound of the water was easiest to ignore, and sat down.

Alistair turned towards the drinks counter, quirking the corners of his mouth down. He'd been telling himself that Raina was just another parent, and this was just another conference, but if he'd been honest with himself he should have expected just this. There was no escaping her small kindnesses, the way that she smoothed his path for him, and it was yet another reason for him to fall in love with her all over again.

CHAPTER TEN

RAINA HADN'T HAD much time to think. New people, new ideas. The conference was one of the better ones she'd been to, and there wasn't a moment that hadn't been filled with the urgent need to ask and answer questions.

Each of the charities that were represented were offered a place in one of the large, bright communal areas to exhibit their work, and today would be spent exchanging ideas and learning from each other. A group of parents from The Watchlight Trust's project were attending for the day, and Raina could see them standing in a tight group, talking only to each other. She looked around for Alistair and Gabriel, but they were busy talking animatedly to the representatives of one of the other charities.

Then she caught sight of Ben, sitting alone in a corner, staring into a cup of coffee, his cheeks red. Raina walked over to him.

'Okay, Ben?'

'Yes. Thanks.' The coffee cup seemed to have replaced his computer monitor as a focus for his attention. Raina sat down, and waited.

'There are some nice ideas here.' If Ben wasn't going to take the hint, she could at least prod him in the right direction.

The mention of ideas always seemed to animate Ben. 'Did you see the one from the group in Norwich?'

'Yes, I did. I think we have a few things to learn from them. I saw you and Alistair talking to them for quite a while.'

Ben nodded. 'That was good. They liked my idea about silicone…'

Raina decided not to enquire about the silicone. Ben was liable to tell her, and the question of what was bothering him would be lost in a flurry of details.

'So what's up, then?'

'The woman over in the corner. She said that I had things all wrong.' Ben flushed again.

Raina looked in the direction he'd indicated. She'd seen the prototype limb and had personally thought it was one of the less imaginative offerings.

'Well, we know we don't have everything

right. That's what makes us work to make the designs better. But you definitely don't have things all wrong, Ben.'

'She said that no one wants things to be too complicated because then they go wrong. And we've had to make a simpler one for Anya as well...'

'That's not because there's anything wrong with the myolectric arm. It's the one that both Alistair and I want her to have, we just have to work up to it a bit.'

'She says she's worked with a lot of different people and she knows just what they want.'

'Well, so have you. You work with Anya.'

Ben gave a shrug. 'Anya's a very cool kid.'

'Yes, I think so too. And I'm glad that's the first thing you see about her, because that's helping you to design a limb that's going to suit her. That's what this is all about, Ben, making limbs that suit individuals and you're doing a great job with Anya.'

'You think so?'

Ben was a genius, but sometimes he didn't have any common sense. And his fascination with the way things worked didn't extend to what made people tick.

'Look, Ben. Did it occur to you that that woman might be feeling that…? Well, she's obviously worked hard and is proud of what she's done. But she might feel that other people have done a bit better than her and instead of trying to learn from them, she's putting them down.'

Ben thought for a moment. 'No. That didn't occur to me.'

The rhetorical question had obviously been a mistake. Raina tried a more direct approach.

Leaning forward, she caught his gaze. 'Don't give up on me, Ben. My cool kid needs a hand, and I'm not going to settle for second best. I want *you* to make her one.'

'You mean you want Alistair to.' Ben's flashes of honesty were often a bit too honest.

'Alistair knows what Anya's medical needs are, but he can't make her a prosthetic. I'm relying on you, Ben, don't let her down. If you do, I'm going to have to have words with you.'

Ben smiled suddenly. 'I won't.'

'Good. Thank you.' Raina nodded towards the group of parents, who'd migrated as one over to the coffee area and were sitting alone, talking. 'We should show them around a bit, and explain what the other projects are doing.'

Ben hesitated. 'What, and let them talk to that woman?' He obviously considered that a return to the lion's den.

'Well, I dare say they'll want to see everything. But if she starts with any of the things she said to you, then I've got a few answers for her.'

Ben looked at her with undisguised admiration. 'You do?'

'Yes, of course I do. And I know for sure that the other parents will back me up.' Raina started to walk across to the group, and realised that Ben hadn't moved. 'Are you coming, then?'

He grinned suddenly. 'Yes. I'm coming.'

One of the things about adjusting to partial deafness was that things became a little more unpredictable. Someone could stand next to him and he wouldn't hear a word they were saying. But sometimes he could catch something from across a crowded room...

Looking at Raina's lips had never been something that Alistair tired of doing. And when he saw her talking to Ben, and her lips formed the shape of his name, warmth had flooded his veins. It was pleasure mixed with pain and regret, because he'd never again be with her in the cool of the night as she whispered his name.

It was probably nothing, a chance comment about work, but he still couldn't get it out of his head. He'd joined the group of parents who were looking around the exhibits, but their questions gave him no chance to speak to Raina. As he dressed for the evening cocktail party, slipping a white shirt over his shoulders, he could almost feel her touch.

The party had already got started, and Gabriel was circulating determinedly. It was a warm night and the glass separating the party space from the central garden had been drawn back. Alistair jumped as he felt a touch on his arm, and a voice said something.

'It's lovely, isn't it.' Raina repeated herself without his having to ask, nodding towards the lights that were beginning to reflect on the water outside.

'Yes.'

It was all he could think of to say. Raina

looked like all his best memories. Only here and now, standing in front of him. He couldn't help but stare and she flushed a little.

'You look…very nice.'

'Thank you.' She looked as awkward about the compliment as he felt. 'Anya told me that I had to wear red and this is my only red dress…'

She remembered too. The dress was sleeveless, plain at the top and falling into pleats at her waist. Raina was wearing the little silver watch that her grandmother had given her. She looked devastatingly gorgeous and the memory of taking that dress off her made Alistair feel dizzy with need.

'She has good taste.' Raina didn't need his permission to wear the dress, but she seemed to want it and she gave a little nod.

'Gabriel's been looking for you.' She twisted round to survey the room and the dress foamed at her knees. Just the way it always had…

'Ah. I'd better go and help him out.'

'Yes. I'll go and see if I can find Ben. He said he wasn't much looking forward to this evening and I said we could face it together.'

That was nice of her. Ben wasn't in his element at parties, and someone to stick with him would stop him from gravitating uncomfortably towards the nearest wall.

He couldn't help it. As they both turned away, he had the opportunity to bend and murmur in her ear. 'I'm glad you kept the dress. You always did look stupendous in it.'

She blushed. Then ran her hand down his lapel, her thumb grazing the fabric of his shirt. He knew that smile. Raina was just as turned on by the compliment as he was.

'I always liked you in a dark suit as well.' She turned suddenly and then she was gone, weaving her way through the groups of people that were forming around them.

He needed a drink. Actually a drink was the last thing he needed. If he was such easy prey to Raina's charms when he was stone-cold sober, then alcohol wasn't a good idea. Alistair made his way over to the bar, asking for a glass of sparkling water, and then went to find Gabriel.

He'd been watching her all evening, and Alistair's growing need to speak to Raina was turning into an emergency. Finally he saw her standing alone. Alistair had lost the thread of the conversation around him about five minutes ago, and it was easy enough to extricate himself and walk across the crowded room to her.

'Would you like to dance?' After-dark piano music was playing lazily, and one end of the space had become an impromptu dance floor.

'Is that…allowed?'

'Why wouldn't it be?'

Raina reddened. 'I'm not sure. Give me a minute to think.'

It was one of the best minutes of Alistair's life. Standing close, warmed by her scent. Watching her eyes, growing darker by the moment. Knowing she wasn't going to come up with a reason.

'We did everything by the book, Raina. Maya chose Anya for the project, and Gabriel's her doctor and signs off on her case files. You don't work for the charity…'

She nudged him. 'I do my share.'

'More than your share, but we don't pay you for it. I think one dance is acceptable.'

'You're my ex-husband.' Something in Raina's eyes told him that that didn't matter. Not tonight.

'Which means I've danced with you before. And there's nothing to say we can't do so again if we want.'

'True.' She stretched up her arms, clasping her hands behind his neck. Giving him the warmth of her body in a way that had always taken Alistair's breath away.

'This is nice.' His body hadn't forgotten her rhythm, even if he'd successfully managed to expunge it from his thoughts.

'Just nice?' Raina knew just as well as he did that *nice* didn't cover it. But, then, no one word did.

'I'm going for understatement. To emphasise my point.'

Raina chuckled. 'In that case, it's just a little bit nice. Maybe...'

'Yeah. Maybe.' He could kiss her now. They were so close, and if he brushed a kiss against her jaw it would look as if he'd simply bent to say something to her as they danced. But Alistair didn't want to. She felt so soft in his arms, and one kiss would never be enough.

Maybe Raina would kiss him. Later on, when it wouldn't matter if he returned the kiss, and made more of it than just a sweet and momentary sensation. For now, the dance was enough.

The party was beginning to break up, and someone had switched off the music. A few stalwarts were sitting at the bar, and Raina imagined they might well be there until the early hours of the morning.

The long, slow dance with Alistair had left her senses reeling. She'd clung to him, unable to let him go, and he'd tucked her hand into the crook of his arm, and they'd walked together out to the far reaches of the garden space, where darkness shrouded them from sight. Tonight had been so perfect, and Raina didn't want it to end.

'Ah!' He let out a long sigh of satisfaction. 'Silence.'

'Silence? Really, Alistair?'

'Yes. At first there were just a few moments, here and there. They got longer, and I still couldn't quite believe it. But my tinnitus has stopped completely now. I haven't heard it for the last two days.'

'That's wonderful. Have you spoken to your audiologist about it?'

He shook his head. 'No, not yet. I don't know whether it'll last, or for how long, so I'm just enjoying it at the moment.'

'I should think that's the only advice your audiologist will give you. No one really understands tinnitus, but this seems like a good sign.'

'Yeah, I think so. And if it does start again, at least I'll know that I enjoyed the silence while it lasted. That was the one thing I couldn't get to grips with, that I'd never appreciated silence before.'

'What else can you hear? Apart from the silence.'

'I can hear…the breeze. Bet you can't hear that.' He smiled at her.

'No, actually I can't. You're hearing it rustle against the back of your hearing aid?'

Alistair nodded. 'I can't hear much else. But that's okay, because I can hear you.'

So he couldn't hear the music, drifting out into the night. Or the quiet sounds of the water. But Alistair didn't seem to feel any loss and right now Raina could understand that. The only thing that mattered right now was the two of them.

She stood on her toes, kissing his cheek. It was full of risk, but that only made her want to do it all the more. He turned, taking her into his arms. They were so warm, and it felt as if she'd spent a very long time out in the cold.

Alistair murmured her name, just once. And then he kissed her.

Raina had just kissed him as if she really meant it. She *did* really mean it, Alistair knew that. It felt as if nothing stood between them now. Not the pain, or the loneliness. Not even the anger over everything that had happened between them.

But if this went on, he wouldn't be able to let her go. He should give her the chance to smile at him, and wish him goodnight, even if it was the last thing he wanted her to do.

'You should go.' His hands felt suddenly cold as he took them from her waist, as if it was only Raina's body heat that had kept him from freezing.

'Do you want me to?' Raina gazed up at him.

'Of course not. That's why you should.' He couldn't take much more of this. Any moment now he'd be on his knees, begging her come back to his room with him and stay the night.

'It's nothing that hasn't happened before…' She used his own argument against him, leaving the conclusion to burst into his thoughts. *There's nothing to say that we can't do it again, if we want to.*

'A lot's happened since then.'

Raina nodded. 'I thought I hated you, but I never did. I couldn't.'

'I thought I hated you too. Turns out that I didn't.' He'd always loved Raina. Always wanted the best for her, even if that meant she should be with someone else.

'We're just too different. That's not going to change, but we could still allow ourselves this. Couldn't we?'

'Yes. I think we could.'

Alistair pulled the keys from his pocket. Along with the key to his room was a master key that would open all the access doors to the building. Putting his arm around her, he led her along the dark path to the door closest to them, which led almost directly to his room.

As soon as they were inside, she flung her arms around his neck. It took an almost superhuman effort to walk the few steps to his room, but somehow he made it, closing the door behind them. He felt the warmth of her body against his, and kissed her again. His limbs begin to shake and Alistair forced himself to think straight.

'Raina… Unless you have condoms…'

'No, I don't. We can improvise, though, can't we?' She licked her lips. Raina had a point. Just the thought of what she could do with her fingers and her mouth was driving him crazy.

'Wait…' He couldn't let her go, even for a moment, and he kissed her all the way to the bathroom door. Flipping open the cabinet, he found what he was looking for. 'I told you this place had everything.'

She snatched the condoms out of his hand, standing on her toes to whisper in his ear. Yes. He wanted to be inside her, too. And yes. For a very long time. His blood felt as if it was starting to boil.

'You're sure, Raina?' He had to know. He had to hear her say it.

She took his head between her hands. 'Yes. I'm sure. Is that enough for you?'

More than enough. He hoisted her up into his arms and made for the bed.

The one thing that Raina had always really liked about Alistair was that as soon as he kicked the bedroom door closed behind him, that easygoing nature of his changed. When he made love, there was no hesitation and no compromise. He understood the fine art of taking it to the limit.

The door was already closed, so there was no kicking needed. But there *was* a bed. As she clung to his neck the years apart seemed to fall away.

He laid her down, undressing her. Letting each scrap of clothing fall to the floor in a calculated act of give and take, which left her shivering with pleasure and anticipation. When he pulled his shirt over his head, disregarding buttons as an unnecessarily indirect route to what they both wanted, Raina smiled.

'You've always been beautiful, Alistair…'

He gave a low growl of humour. 'A little older. You, on the other hand, don't get old. Just more exquisite.'

'Older suits you.' His body was a little heavier,

but every inch of it was muscle and strength. He'd been taking really good care of himself while she'd been gone.

She wondered whether he'd take the hearing aid out, and he did. It was the one thing he didn't fling aside, laying it carefully on the table beside the bed. Then he lay down beside her, holding her tight against the taut strength of his body.

'I want to hear you, Raina. Every breath. Every word…'

That meant face to face. Staring into each other's eyes as they made love. Looking for the clues that told them that they hadn't forgotten how to nurture sensation until it exploded between them, out of control.

'I want to hear you too, Alistair.'

He eased his body over hers, and Raina clung to him, feeling his hand move across her thighs and between her legs. So gentle, and yet with the ultimate promise of such fierce pleasure.

The one thing that never changed was the bond that had been forged in their eyes. Alistair's gaze never left hers as their bodies moved, and he saw everything that she felt. It was a precious link, born of necessity, which became a thing of delight.

'What you said, Raina... About having me inside you for a long time...'

'That'll be next time...'

He grinned down at her, watching her face as he moved. Raina wound her legs around his waist, twisting her body, and he groaned. Everything they'd ever had together, pleasure and loss, anger and love, melted together and drove them on.

She felt the orgasm begin to build. He knew, and she knew that he was close too. Suddenly there was only Alistair, and the unstoppable joy of completion. He cried out and she held him tight.

He kissed her, laying his forehead against hers, while they both got their breath back. Then he chuckled, rolling onto his back, taking her with him in an embrace.

'I never thought we'd do that again.' Finally he spoke.

'Me neither. I'm glad we did.'

Raina stretched up to kiss him and then turned in his arms, so that he could curl his body around hers. Alistair pulled the duvet across them both, holding her tight.

Suddenly she was alone with her thoughts. Being with Alistair had made the whole world recede. Nothing could touch them, and they had no interest in touching anything but each other. But now, in the quiet peace after the storm, everything started to filter back and it was just as it had been before.

They still couldn't be together, they'd been through too much for that. This had just been a way of letting go.

She was crying. Somehow Alistair sensed it even if Raina's body was still, pressed against his chest. He probably wouldn't be able to hear if she said something, and he felt entirely at sea. His body still buzzed with the pleasure of making love to her, and the sudden, hedonistic joy of its climax.

Perhaps he should leave her alone with her thoughts. If she wanted to tell him, she would. But the sudden thought that she might be regretting what they'd just done tore at him.

'Raina… Are you awake?' He whispered the words softly. For a moment she lay still and then he felt her squeeze his hand. When she turned in his arms, her face was composed.

'Raina, honey. What's the matter? Did I hurt you?'

'No. Everything's okay.'

That was his line. He suddenly realised how much it hurt to hear it, when he knew that something was wrong.

'No, it's not. I'm not going to leave you alone until you talk to me. Then I'll talk to you in return.' Alistair reached for his hearing aid, wanting to hear everything that she said. But she laid her hand on his, taking the hearing aid away from him.

'Are you up for doing this the other way?' She gave him a smile and sat up, operating the remote beside the bed to turn the lights up a little and facing him.

Alistair wasn't sure. Words would have to be spoken plainly and clearly, within the bonds of their exchanged gaze. But if they could do it while they were making love, then they could do it now. He sat up, holding his hand out towards her. She reached out, placing her palm against his. It was electric.

'Do you mind?'

He shook his head. 'No. I always used to leave the talking to you. Far more than I should have done.'

She nodded. 'Is that different now?'

'No. I'm no different. But I want to be.' He leaned towards her, tracing his fingers gently across her jaw. 'Raina, please tell me. I need to know what's going on because you seem... hurt.'

'You didn't hurt me. I...' She turned away from him, then seemed to remember that she had to face him. Making sure that he heard had become secondary. This was about making sure that they both understood.

'Everything we lost. It just suddenly felt very real to me.'

'Me too.' Alistair turned the corners of his mouth down. 'You know, I always thought that you'd find someone else. Someone who'd do a little better than I did in giving you the things you wanted.'

'What things do you mean? Children?' Her eyes glistened with tears.

'That was my main thought, yes.' It was the one that had carried Alistair through. The idea that someone, somewhere would make a great father to her children. If Raina had what she wanted then it made all of the misery seem like a price that had to be paid, and not just meaningless.

'I can't have children, Alistair. Or…at least probably not.' She must see the shock in his face, and Alistair struggled not to turn away from her and hide. 'When I lost our baby…'

She couldn't say the words and he had to help her. Alistair took a deep breath. 'An ectopic pregnancy doesn't usually mean that you can't conceive again.'

'No, but I started to experience pain, and so I went for some tests. It turned out that there was an infection and they had to remove one fallopian tube. The other is partially blocked.'

Just one question pounded in Alistair's brain. 'When did this happen, Raina?'

'About a year after I lost the baby.'

A year. He and Raina had still been married then. Not living together any more, and they had been just a pen-stroke away from divorce, but they'd still been married. 'And…you didn't tell me?'

'Would you have signed the divorce papers if I had?'

No, probably not. He stared at her dumbfounded. Then, as he looked away, he was aware that she'd said something. He felt her finger on his jaw, tipping his head back towards her.

'Did you hear that?'

Alistair shook his head.

'I said that we'd made our decision about divorcing. The best thing for both of us was to get it done, and go on with our lives.'

'But…you could have told me, Raina.' He looked away from her, not wanting to hear her answer. He knew full well why she hadn't told him. He'd struggled to support her through the loss of their baby, knowing he was making a poor job of it, and there was no reason why this should have been any different.

She'd ripped away the security blanket that he'd wrapped around himself. Raina going on with her life. Meeting someone, and then becoming a wife and a mother. Being fulfilled in her career, and happy until the day she died. It was a rose-tinted view of life, but it was the one that worked for him.

The truth had been so different. Her dreams

had been shattered and then she'd weathered unimaginable tragedy. All she had was Anya now, and Alistair silently sent up a vote of thanks to the little girl, for every time she'd made Raina smile.

'May I hold you?' It was the only thing he could think of to do.

'Yes. I'd really like that.' She wrapped her arms around his neck, pulling him down onto the bed. Face to face this time. Her head on the pillow next to his. They were both tangled up in the duvet and he couldn't slide his hand around her waist and embrace her the way he would have liked, but this was…enough. Better, maybe.

'I'm so sorry, Raina.'

'You have nothing to be sorry for. We both had our own ways of surviving, and they were different. We both needed to be apart.'

'So where does that leave us now?' Alistair hoped that Raina had some clue about that, because he had none.

She was thinking hard. 'I guess…lots of people divorce and stay on good terms.'

'Exes with benefits, you mean?'

'No! That sounds too cynical. You're a lot more to me than just a romp between the sheets whenever I feel like it.' She dug her fingers into his ribs.

'You're a lot more than that to me, too.' Alistair picked up her hand, kissing her fingertips. 'Friends?'

'Yes. Friends is good.'

'Along with the proviso that if you *do* feel like a romp between the sheets, you can always pick up the phone. I'm at your beck and call.'

Raina smirked. 'Apart from when you're working, that is.' There was a note of irony in her tone.

'I guess so. Some things don't change all that much.'

Raina smiled at him. 'I don't suppose you're free now, are you?'

'Nothing in the diary.'

'There's nothing in mine either.' She snuggled close, kissing him. 'Which means that you're at my beck and call, then?'

'I'd *love* to be at your beck and call.'

They made love again. Tenderly at first, and then with the increasing fervour that Alistair did so well. Somehow, it felt as if the unfinished business of the past was being swept away. If they couldn't live together, then maybe this was their way of learning how to live better apart.

'You're hungry?' He found an empty table in the crowded restaurant, and they both sat down. No thought of taking this last chance of talking to the other delegates before everyone left for home, they only had eyes for each other.

'I could work my way through the whole menu.' Raina smiled at him. Alistair knew exactly what that meant. They'd always joked that great sex deserved a hearty breakfast.

'I could too.'

The noise around them made it difficult to talk. But words weren't necessary. They both tucked into a full English breakfast, stopping only to exchange smiles.

But gradually the world at large began to intrude. By the time they'd finished their second cup of coffee, people had started to approach Alistair to shake his hand and thank him for a great two days. Maya came to sit at their table, ordering toast and asking Raina about Anya's progress.

Raina left Alistair in the bustle of the reception area to go to her room and pack. And then there was no opportunity to speak with him privately. Alistair had torn himself away from a minor crisis involving a flat tyre on someone's car, and met her as she prepared to leave.

'Safe home.' He walked her out of the building, to her car.

'You too. I hope you get everything sorted.' Raina nodded across to the group of people around the stricken car.

'It'll be okay. We've called the local garage, and they're on their way.' He caught her arm. 'I have no regrets, Raina. I hope you don't either.'

'None. I'll see you tomorrow? I'm coming into the office for a meeting with Ben.'

He smiled. 'I look forward to it.'

As she drove away, Raina saw him standing in the car park, watching her go.

The drive home had allowed her some time to think. But when Raina shut her front door behind her, leaning against it as if to reassure herself that she was truly alone, she still hadn't come to any conclusions.

'What have I done?' She asked the question, but there was no answer from the empty hallway. Undeterred, Raina continued the conversation.

'It's just...*lust*.'

No, it wasn't. If last night had just been lust then it wouldn't be so complicated. They'd looked into each other's eyes. She'd told him things that she'd thought she never would. It was only after they'd cleared the air that she'd truly given herself to him, and he'd given himself back.

Unfinished business.

The inescapable conclusion was beginning to haunt Raina. She'd thought that Alistair inhabited a world of regrets that were well and truly in her past. But she'd come to realise that they'd both been blinkered. Neither of them had been able to see past the pain of losing their baby and their divorce, and it was only now that each was able to see how the other had been feeling.

Maybe they could rewrite their own story. Bring it to a close and allow themselves to move on. Because moving on was really the only thing they could do now.

Raina picked up her case, hauling it up the stairs. She needed to wash Alistair's scent from her body, and change her clothes. And then she needed to go and pick Anya up from her parents' house and get on with her life.

CHAPTER ELEVEN

ALISTAIR WAS BROODING in his office. It was tough to brood after what had happened between him and Raina. Edward was sitting on his desk, ready to show the next child how his tiny prosthetic arm worked, and he wanted to make a high five with the bear.

He'd seen Raina briefly when she'd popped her head around his office door on her way up to see Ben. Alistair had been careful to treat her exactly as he would if that last night at the conference hadn't happened. Not too forward. Not too restrained either. She'd obviously been doing the same and it had shown. Doing what came naturally didn't seem quite so natural when you were thinking about it.

Maybe they'd just pretend that it had never happened. But Raina's admission that it was unlikely that she'd have children of her own had altered their shared history. And anyone who'd ever seen a film that dealt with time travel knew that one small alteration in the timeline could trickle down to the present day, changing everything.

He saw Raina walk through the outer office just as the last of the staff were getting ready to leave. She was wearing a yellow top today, a bright sunflower hue, which suited her. She was also wearing a worried expression.

'How did it go with Ben?' Alistair decided to load the responsibility for Raina's obvious discomfiture onto Ben's shoulders.

'Okay... It's been a long day.' She plumped herself down in the chair opposite his desk, dumping the untidy mass of papers that she'd been carrying onto her lap.

'That doesn't sound as good as it might have been.' Alistair nodded towards the papers. 'I see you've taken a few notes.'

Raina rolled her eyes. 'Ben's great, and he's trying really hard. He just finds it difficult to distil everything down into a simple overview of the system. Look, he's printed out a copy of the user manual for the software for me. And he's made a few useful annotations...'

Alistair chuckled. 'Do you want me to have a word with him?'

'No, that's okay. I challenged him to write a one-page summary of what the software can do, and encouraged him to use bullet points. I don't see how he can confuse me too much with that.'

'Did you specify font size?' Alistair knew that Ben's ingenuity would probably find a way of getting around the limitations that *one page* would put on him.

'No, I didn't.' Raina frowned. 'I said it had to be readable, so let's hope he takes the hint and doesn't make the text so small I can't see it. And I told him that what's blindingly obvious to him needs a bit of explaining to ordinary mortals like me, so he needs to start with the basics.'

Raina thought she was an ordinary mortal? She was sunshine, and the cool, fresh touch of dew. She was a warrior champion for her daughter, and extraordinary in every way.

'You underestimate yourself.'

Her gaze met his and suddenly the full impact of their night together hit Alistair. What they could have done, if only they hadn't given up on their marriage. History readjusted itself, and he felt the ripples wash over him.

'It's good of you to say so. I hope you're right.' She looked down at the pile of papers in her lap.

'I think you're one of the few people who can take Ben on and win.' Alistair heard the tenderness in his own voice and tried to swallow it down. What he was about to suggest had nothing to do with their relationship, and it was best he make that clear. 'Gabriel had a suggestion...'

Raina nodded, seeming to catch the unspoken implication. 'What's that?'

'He thinks it's too much to ask that you do all the preparatory work and hold sessions for new parents for free. I agree with him, and we've put together a draft job description. We can pay you an hourly rate, and you can work whenever you want.'

He pushed the typed sheet across his desk, and Raina picked it up, studying it. Perhaps he should have said that *Gabriel* had drafted the job description. But there was only so much distancing that Alistair could do before it started to look too obvious.

Raina put the paper back down onto his desk. 'It's a really good overview of what I need to do, and I'd like to keep that. But I'd feel more comfortable with donating my time, at least for starters.'

Maybe Raina was happier with an arrangement that didn't make him her boss. Alistair could concur with that.

'It's not within my remit as a director of this charity to force the money on you.' Alistair applied his mind to the problem. 'Maybe we could help you by providing childcare for Anya. It's something we'd need to look into for the parents who'll be attending these sessions with you.'

'Yes… Yes, that would be great. My mum will always take her, but I'd prefer not to rely on her. And Anya loves coming here.'

'Okay. We'll do that then. But if the project really takes off then your role will expand with it. If you're doing more than one day's work a week, we'll be insisting that you consider taking a salary.'

Raina nodded. Now was about the time that she should be getting up from her seat and telling him that she had to go and pick Anya up. They'd said all they had to say about the business side of things, and there was no excuse for Alistair to keep her here, and none for Raina to stay.

All the same, she didn't move. And neither did he.

It was awkward. And it wasn't like Raina. She'd always been so ready to tell him what was on her mind and how she was feeling, and sometimes Alistair felt that she jumped straight in without really thinking about it. He, on the other hand, thought about it so much that he usually didn't get around to saying anything.

But things could change. Alistair took a breath.

'Raina. About the other night...'

She looked up at him far too quickly. And the sudden blush on her cheeks told him that she'd been thinking about that too. He swallowed hard, making an effort to collect his thoughts.

'Raina, I don't want to pretend it didn't happen because...what we shared was important.' He glanced at her and she nodded. No need to elaborate, she knew what he was talking about. 'Whatever happens next is fine by me.'

She was looking at him steadily. 'What *will* happen next?'

'I have no clue.' Alistair rubbed his hands

across his face. 'But I won't regret any of it, because I feel that we cleared the air between us a little.'

'And the sex was pretty great. The best, actually...' This was the old Raina. The one who said exactly what she was thinking as soon as it came to mind and she accompanied it with a sudden, mischievous grin.

'It pretty much redefined the meaning of best...' Alistair ventured a compliment that was really only the truth, and Raina shot him a look of delighted glee.

This was about as much of an inquest on the night before as Alistair could cope with. He got to his feet awkwardly, and Raina followed his lead. 'I'd better be going. I need to pick up Anya.'

'Sure. You'll be back to take another run at Ben tomorrow?'

'What, you think he's got me beaten already?' Their conversation had done one thing at least. Raina had lost the air of dejection that she'd had when she'd walked into his office.

'The idea never crossed my mind.' Alistair chuckled, opening the door of his office for her. As Raina walked past him, she glanced outside at the empty workspace and turned quickly, brushing a kiss onto his cheek.

'Thanks for the talk. Especially the part about redefining best...' She murmured the words and then she was gone.

Alistair slowly raised his fingers to his cheek. He could no longer convince himself that he'd take what they had and be content if it never happened again. Every part of him wanted more.

They were like flies, caught in amber. Raina was afraid to go on, but she didn't want to go back either. Alistair had made no move, and perhaps he was feeling as confused as she was.

Concentrating on the task in hand helped take her mind off it all. After her second session with Ben, she felt able to write a basic overview of how the computer system worked, and what it could provide. Now she could move on to medical and social issues, which she felt much more at home with.

It was fun as well. Working on this stretched her in a way that she'd missed since she'd given up work to look after Anya.

Anya was learning how to make the most

from her new prosthetics. She still used the fixed hand for rough and tumble games, so that the myolectric one wasn't damaged, but Kaia had begun to teach her how to use the myolectric hand for more complex tasks.

It was becoming the norm that she'd walk into Alistair's office and find that he and Anya were taking a break from the serious business of the day and concentrating on building castles. When she walked into his office, two faces looked up at her with exactly the same expressions.

Only Anya voiced the disappointment. 'I don't want to go, Mum…'

'We'll be back tomorrow.' Two faces brightened at the prospect, Alistair's a little more because he had a firmer grasp on the reality of tomorrow.

'But my castle…' Anya stuck her bottom lip out.

'Alistair will keep your castle safe for you. It'll be here.'

That wasn't Anya's concern. She got to her feet, walking carefully around the half-built fairy castle made from sparkly bricks, and put her small hand on the side of Alistair's face, tipping it towards her.

'Can you hear me?'

'Yes, I can hear you, Anya.' Alistair was trying to suppress a smile and failing miserably. Anya's insistence that he hear everything she said was something that seemed precious to him.

'Don't play with my castle when I'm not here.'

'No, Anya. I won't.'

'Promise!'

Alistair nodded solemnly, putting his hand on his heart. 'I promise.'

Clearly suspecting the same as Raina, that the promise might be a hard one for him to keep, Anya tugged at his arm, and Alistair got to his feet. Pulling him away from the castle, and to the other side of his desk, she pushed him into his chair.

A tall, powerful man entirely at the mercy of a child. Anya wasn't just another child that The Watchlight Trust could help, he was falling in love. Raina blinked tears from her eyes as she bent down, lifting the castle carefully and putting it on top of the filing cabinet. Alistair stayed put, grinning, while Anya helped her scoop the bricks on the floor back into the bucket.

'Shall we take your magic hand off now?' The fixed hand was much lighter for Anya to wear.

'I want it on me. In the car.'

Raina glanced in Alistair's direction and he nodded. 'All right, sweetie. Go and say goodbye to Heidi.'

Anya ran from the room, and Heidi turned her swivel chair to give the little girl a hug goodbye, and a sweet from the jar on her desk.

'How is she doing?'

Alistair frowned. 'Kaia's made a lot of progress with her, but she's still using the hand as a scoop. She's having a bit of trouble using the muscles in her arm to move the fingers.'

Raina held up her little finger, wiggling it. 'But she's managed to get *you* wrapped round this one.'

'Nonsense.' Alistair took a shot at an unconvincing denial, and then smiled. 'I'll see you both tomorrow.'

The next day, Raina spent the afternoon alone in the conference room, putting the finishing touches to her induction talk. Time ran away with her, and when she returned to the main office, she found that Kaia had finished her session with Anya, and Alistair was babysitting. She could see him through the glass partition, sitting on the sofa with his feet propped up on the coffee table. Anya was sitting next to him, her head resting against his chest, and Heidi shot Raina a grin, beckoning her over to her desk.

'How long have they been doing that for?' Alistair had stretched out his left hand in front of Anya, and was curling the fingers one by one. She mimicked the action with her own fingers. Then the harder part. He extended his right hand, moving his thumb. Anya frowned, trying to emulate the movement with her prosthetic.

'Oh, about half an hour.' Heidi grinned, shooting Raina a knowing look. 'You can't help liking a man who's good with kids, can you?'

'No. You can't.' Especially a man who was good with *her* child. And more particularly when it was Alistair...

A child's shriek of delight came from the

office. Anya had moved the thumb of her prosthetic and Alistair was grinning at her. She reached up, tapping his face and giving an instruction that Raina couldn't hear. But she knew what it was. *Again...*

Alistair nodded, stretching out his hand again and moving his thumb. Anya copied the movement perfectly this time, and Alistair nodded, giving her a luminous smile.

'Would you like some coffee, Heidi?' The temptation to rush into the office, catch her little girl into her arms and hug her was pounding at her heart. But this was Alistair's moment. He'd worked hard for it, and it was a shared triumph for him and Anya that Raina didn't want to take away from them.

'Don't you want to…?' Heidi gestured towards the office, and then smiled. 'Yeah, it would be a shame to disturb them. And I could do with a coffee. Thanks.'

As she made the drinks, Raina glanced back at Alistair. He wasn't pushing things, knowing that if he did Anya might reject the work they'd already done. He had one of the sparkly bricks in his hand and was fiddling with it absently as he talked to Anya.

He reached for the story book that was tucked down the side of the sofa, and offered it to Anya. The little girl had become used to the way that Alistair encouraged her to pass all kinds of objects back and forth between them, and she opened the book, giving it back to him so he could read to her.

Heidi nodded her thanks without even looking at Raina as she placed the coffee on her desk. Alistair and Anya seemed unaware that anyone was watching, completely wrapped up in their own world. Alistair dropped the brick on the open pages of the book, and picked it up again.

'Oh, for goodness' sake.' Heidi whispered the words. 'I wouldn't have the patience. Is this killing you?'

'Yep.' All the same, Raina didn't move. If she interrupted them now, Alistair would have to start all over again.

He dropped the brick again, and Anya reached for it. But he was too quick for her, picking it up and continuing with the story. When he dropped it again, Anya batted his hand away, and he coiled his fingers gently around her right arm, so that she'd have to use the prosthetic to pick the brick up if she wanted it. His smile indicated that this was all just a game.

Raina felt Heidi's hand in hers, and she gripped it tightly. Heidi seemed to be holding her breath too as Anya reached with the prosthetic, clumsily moving the thumb, so that she could pick the brick up.

'Nice one, Anya.' Heidi murmured the words. Raina heard Alistair's exclamation of approval, and he hugged Anya.

He held out his hand, and Anya opened her hand to put the brick into his. Then he dropped it, and she picked it up again.

'She's got it...' Raina breathed the words softly.

'Go in...go in.' Heidi squeezed her hand.

'No, I... I don't want to disturb them.'

'They've done it, Raina. Go and share it.'

The thought that Alistair might want to share this achievement with her, as much as she did with him, brought a lump to Raina's throat. Suddenly he looked up and saw her, and beckoned her in. Heidi gave her a push, and she hurried into the office, stopping short in front of them.

'Shall we show Mummy?' Alistair looked up at her, smiling, and Anya nodded. He held out his hand for the brick and the two of them went through the process of dropping it and picking it up again.

'That's so clever of you, sweetie...' Tears suddenly spilled from Raina's eyes, and Anya looked at her questioningly.

'Are you sad, Mummy?'

'No, Anya. I'm happy to see what a clever girl you are.' Raina wiped away the tears, and smiled at her daughter. Anya accepted the information as just another random thing that adults did, and went back to playing with the brick, passing it carefully from one hand to the other.

Alistair let her continue with the game for a while, as Raina watched. Then he got to his feet, taking Anya with him and delivering her into Raina's arms for a hug. For one moment, it seemed as if he was about to put his arms around them both, and it felt like everything she'd ever wanted.

Then he drew back. Collecting up the bricks and the storybook, and putting them on the top of the filing cabinet, next to the castle, which was almost finished now, Raina mouthed words of thanks to him and he smiled, sitting down behind his desk.

'You want to go home now?' Anya seemed tired after the afternoon's session.

'Are we coming back tomorrow?'

'No, tomorrow's Saturday. We'll come back on Monday.' Raina set Anya back on her feet. 'Go and say goodbye to Heidi. I expect she's got a sweet for you.'

Anya ran out to Heidi's desk, and Heidi produced two sweets, one for each hand. Raina turned to Alistair, wondering how she was going to resist hugging him.

'How's the talk going?' He was still safely behind his desk and Raina dropped into the chair on the other side.

'Great. I've pretty much finished now. I'll be looking for someone to try it out on next week.'

Alistair paused then seemed to come to a decision. 'I'm not doing anything at the weekend. If you and Anya would like to come over for lunch on Saturday, we could have a play session and you could try the talk out on me.'

It was *very* tempting. 'But you know it all already.'

'Yes, and I know the kind of questions that people ask. I can throw those at you and see if I can trip you up. And I don't know it all, I never did get around to having Ben give me an overview of how the computer system works. I just point at things and he tells me whether he can do it or not.'

'Oh! So you decided to pass the problem over to me, did you?'

Alistair nodded. 'I thought you'd make a much better job of it than I can. And you know Ben. He prefers to stare at the computer screen while he's talking to you.'

'You could handle that now.' Alistair had made good progress with the hearing aid, and hardly ever missed what people were saying to him. If he did, it wasn't a matter of concern to him any more, he just asked them to repeat themselves.

'I just want to hear it from you.' He stretched his arms, as if this new ability to reach out had extended to the physical world. 'You're the one who's going to be running the induction course. And you're a lot prettier than Ben, so I'll be hanging on every word you say.'

That did it. Practicality was one thing, but she couldn't resist the look in his eyes.

'What time?' Raina pulled out her phone to make a note in her calendar and then quirked her lips down. 'I'm sorry… I completely forgot it was the third Saturday in the month. Mum has a sleepover for Anya and I'm taking her over there at lunchtime.'

'Then how about dinner? If you don't have any plans yourself.'

Alistair had given her a way out. She could say that she was doing something and walk away. But Saturday evening on her own, when she could be spending it with Alistair, sounded impossibly dreary.

'Dinner would be great, thank you. I'll bring my visual aids with me and we can see if they pass muster.'

CHAPTER TWELVE

ALISTAIR'S HOUSE WAS in a quiet road in Muswell Hill. Raina's hand was trembling as she pressed the doorbell, and saw his shadow through the stained glass in the front door.

'Hi. You made it.' He opened the door, standing back to let her inside.

There had always been a chance that she wouldn't. Last night she'd woken up more than once and made the decision that she'd cancel, only to change her mind and decide to go. He seemed to know that.

Raina stepped into the hall, looking around. The house was one of many in the area that dated back to the early nineteen-hundreds, and this one had escaped the over-zealous modifications that had spoiled so many of its type. Floor tiles in terracotta, blue and cream were laid in an intricate pattern of squares and triangles all the way along the hall, and when Alistair led her into the sitting room, a well-polished cast-iron fireplace, framed with a carved wooden surround, caught her eye.

'This is really nice.' The room was spacious, with a high ceiling, and decorated in neutral colours to accentuate the grace of the moulded plasterwork and the panelled door. 'I wish I had some of these period features.'

He winced, as if the comparison between her place and his made him uncomfortable. 'My wish is that I could make this into a real home. Like yours…'

Raina looked around. 'Well, maybe it could do with a few finishing touches.'

'I thought I *had* finished until I visited you. Then I realised I hadn't.'

It had been this way before. Alistair's love of clean lines and hers of clutter had somehow managed to combine into warmth with an air of order and sophistication. Raina had loved the house they'd had when they were married, and had never quite managed to re-create the look in her cottage.

But that had been then. And now they both had to make do with half of a whole that had seemed so perfect for a while. 'So tell me. How did you manage to find a place that still had the fireplace and all the plaster mouldings intact?'

'It took me a while.' Alistair looked around the room as if he were assessing it for the first time. 'When I did, it needed a bit of restoration.'

'You did this yourself?' Alistair wasn't a born handyman, but he'd had five years to learn.

'No.' He shot her a pained look. 'I was practically living at work, and I left it to the builders.'

That sounded a bit more like it. 'So you don't have any tips on stripping a fireplace?' Raina ran her hand across the smooth, polished wood of the mantelpiece. It was undoubtedly original, and the small imperfections of age only added to its appeal.

'Not one. My builder did a great job, and I left him to it. The only thing I'd have contributed to the process would have been unwelcome interference.'

Raina chuckled. 'Okay. I'm reassured that you haven't undergone a complete personality transplant.'

'I haven't changed that much. Just deafer and with a few more grey hairs…'

If he had any grey hairs, Raina couldn't see them. Alistair was the picture of a man who was just starting to reach his prime. His polo shirt and jeans did little to conceal the strong lines of his body, and if his face seemed more assured, then his tawny eyes were the same. Capable of an irresistible boyishness when he smiled, even if they did seem to hold a hint of sadness at times. Maybe hers did too. They'd both seen their share of grief.

'So…' Alistair rubbed his hands together, seeming to prefer action to speculation. 'Dinner's prepared and it won't take more than twenty minutes to cook. What do you think— we can do the talk now, then eat and discuss it all afterwards?'

'That sounds perfect. I tell you how things are supposed to work, and then you ask a few awkward questions.'

His grin showed a trace of mischief. 'Sounds like a plan.'

There was no plan. Just the two of them, and an evening that could finish any way they wanted it to. Whatever it held, she was ready.

* * *

Alistair had brought the data projector home from work, and with a little fiddling around Raina hooked it up to her laptop. He moved the sofa, giving her a blank wall for the projected images, and then closed the curtains and settled himself into an armchair. Raina shot him a slightly embarrassed smile and then began.

She had nothing to be embarrassed about. Her presentation was clear and understandable, and she covered all the issues. When she got to the part about the computer system, Alistair found that Raina had done the impossible and reduced what both he and Gabriel had dismissed as being way above their heads to something that seemed easy.

'Any questions?'

'Nope.'

Raina frowned. 'Is that because you understand everything? Or because it's all as clear as mud?'

'I've got it. It all makes perfect sense.' His answer didn't seem to mollify Raina, and Alistair tried to think of something to say. 'All right. So the size of the prosthesis is just scaled up or down to fit the individual child, is it?'

'You know very well that it isn't, but it's the kind of question someone might ask…' Raina smirked with satisfaction and warmth tingled through his chest. He didn't remember having a crush on any of his teachers when he was a child, but he was making up for it now. The chance to watch her unashamedly, to react to everything she said, was affecting him far more than he'd thought it might.

She pulled up another set of images from her laptop, and launched into an explanation of how each prosthetic was tailored to fit an individual child. This had clearly caught her imagination and her enthusiasm shone through her words. Since Alistair already knew the process, he allowed himself to forget what she was saying and watch Raina.

'I wouldn't normally include the part about how the team use the software to do it, but when Ben showed me, it was fascinating. Does it make sense?'

'Uh…? Yes, I see it.' The way that Raina moved made sense. He could understand exactly why the shadows in the room would want to caress her face. 'It's a beautiful concept.'

She smiled. 'Yes, it is, isn't it? That's the way

that Ben sees it, and when he gets cross and waves people away is when he thinks they're not appreciating it properly.'

Ben could be in love with the concept if he wanted, that was his choice. Alistair preferred to be in love with the teacher.

He dismissed the thought, because being in love with Raina had a lot of complications attached to it, ones that the finest mind wouldn't be able to make sense of. 'So is this a good time to break for dinner?'

'Yes.' Raina shot him a look of mock solemnity, which made his heart bounce in his chest. 'Afterwards you can think up a few more tricky questions for me.'

Dinner was a couple of pan-sizzled steaks, done the way that Raina liked them, with peppercorn sauce. Alistair had decided that the table in the breakfast room lent the right amount of informality to the meal, but had made the concession of covering it with a white cloth and adding a couple of candles and a bottle of very good red wine. Two mixed salads were placed on the table, and he dimmed the lights as far as he dared. Nice, but not romantic.

Raina's presence was something he hadn't calculated in, though. He'd always felt that she could turn a sandwich on a park bench in November into an intimate, romantic meal for two, and this was no challenge to her at all.

'Would you like some more wine?' Alistair didn't refill his own glass. One had already gone to his head.

'No, thanks. Half a glass is enough for me. I'm driving, remember...'

Yes, of course. He'd almost forgotten that Raina had her own home and that she'd be going back there tonight. 'I'll make some coffee, then.'

He walked through the wide arch and down the step that led into the kitchen. Turning the lights on full to make the coffee didn't make the slightest difference. Raina was just as beautiful as she'd been by candlelight.

He made the coffee good and strong, to bring him to his senses. There was still work to do this evening. But the spell still lingered, and when he sat back down at the table and poured the coffee, he couldn't help it. This had been bugging him for too many years.

'Do you mind if I ask you something?'

'No, of course not. About the computer system?'

He shook his head. 'No.'

She took a sip of her coffee and glanced up at him. Maybe she saw Alistair's hesitancy, because her eyes darkened suddenly. 'Ask me anything.'

'It's about…what happened. Six years ago.' Maybe Raina had put that in the past now, and she didn't want to revive it. He should give her the chance to shut him down.

'Go on.'

'Did you feel…? Did *I* make you feel that I didn't care? When we lost the baby.'

She clasped her hands together, her gaze falling to the tablecloth. 'You didn't make me feel anything, Alistair. I felt the things I felt all by myself.'

No. If Raina was blaming herself for anything that had happened then she could stop. Right now.

'I never told you, Raina. What else could you be expected to think?'

Suddenly her gaze was on him, seeming to devour him in its intensity. 'You said that you felt guilty…about not being there when I lost the baby. And I told you that there was nothing you could have done.'

That had hurt. The thought that he was of so little use to her that it hadn't mattered whether he was there or not. Alistair bit back the pain. 'Yes?'

'I lied. I needed you there so badly, Alistair. I was just afraid to admit it.'

A feeling of warmth spread across his chest. Raina *had* wanted him. But then the sick feeling of guilt reasserted itself. 'I wasn't there, though.'

'If you'd known, you would have been. I blamed you for not caring enough about our child, but I know that was wrong of me.' Raina stretched out her hand, letting her fingertips touch his. 'I know that you grieved as much as I did.'

Alistair swallowed hard. But this was what he'd done all along, swallowed down his feelings, and it had done them both such damage.

'I felt…unequal to it all. Helpless. You were so unhappy and I didn't know how to make things better for you.' He moved his hand, tangling his fingers with hers. 'I really wanted our child, but I was just worried. That I'd be a terrible father.'

'You…?' Raina looked shocked. 'What made you think that?'

'I wanted to give you everything, but we didn't have much money to spare at that point, and I couldn't see how I'd be able to provide for you and our child without turning into the kind of father who's never there.' Alistair shrugged. 'Like my father.'

She stared at him uncomprehendingly. 'You never talked much about your father, Alistair.'

Yeah. One of the many things he'd chosen not to talk about. 'There isn't a lot to say. He had his own business, and worked all hours. We had a great childhood, he provided us with everything that money could buy. Apart from himself, that is.'

'You never saw him?'

Alistair huffed out a laugh that wasn't really a laugh at all. 'Put it like this. When we were teenagers, my brother and I had a joke. We reckoned that it was impossible that my father could have been home for long enough to conceive five children, and that at least one of us must owe our existence to our father having…posted his contribution to the process to our mother in an envelope.'

Raina giggled suddenly. 'I bet you didn't put it quite so delicately…'

'No, we didn't. Rob was fifteen at the time and determined to make it quite clear to me that he knew all about those things.'

'So…did you ever decide which one of you owed their existence to an envelope?' Raina was teasing him now and it felt like a cool salve applied to an inflamed nerve.

'Rachel.'

'No! Poor Rachel!' Her hand flew to her mouth and then he saw realisation in her eyes. 'That wasn't what you all found so funny at our wedding, was it? When Rachel handed you an empty envelope, and the three of you cracked up. You said it was nothing…'

Alistair chuckled. That had been a good day. 'You had enough on your hands with your dress, remember?'

'Yes, I remember. It was just as well that your mother happened to have a safety pin on her.'

'Mum always just happens to have a safety

pin on her. Along with anything else that might come in handy.' The warmth of that day was almost palpable now. The remembered happiness, which hadn't yet been soured by the pain.

'I'm beginning to get into the way of that myself, with Anya. There are never too many useful things you can have in your handbag. How your mum ever managed with five of you… You never said, Alistair. About your father.'

'It always seemed a bit like tempting fate to me. My mother always used to tell me that I was like him.'

'Maybe to give you some feeling of connection with him.' Raina pursed her lips.

'Yeah, maybe. Maybe because I *am* like him. You know, when he died, I couldn't think of anything concrete that I might miss about him.' Life had carried on in their household in much the same way. When Rob had gone to university the following year, he'd felt more in the way of loss.

'Just the things you didn't have.'

'Yeah, I suppose so.' Alistair shook his head. Their talk hadn't been so bad—at least not so far. They hadn't argued, and they'd laid a few more of the ghosts of the past to rest. They should probably stop now. Get out while the going was good.

'More coffee? Or are you ready for the questions?'

Raina nodded. 'More coffee. While you make it, I'll go and get my laptop, I've got some more detailed graphics that explain the various points I made in my talk…'

Suddenly she reached out, gripping his hand. 'You're not your father, Alistair. You should know that. One day you'll make a great dad.'

But not with *her*. And that took all the allure away from the prospect. He and Raina might be friends, they might even be casual lovers, but they'd ruled out the idea of ever making a life together again.

He shook his head and she quirked her lips down. Nothing more was needed. They both knew that he couldn't change who he was.

Better make the best of it, then. Alistair smiled, rising from his seat, and started to clear the table.

They'd said the things that should have been said six years ago. Every time they talked, the hurt seemed to lift a little more from Raina's heart, and it became so much easier to love Alistair again.

Raina sat down at the table and opened her laptop with trembling fingers. She knew how she wanted the evening to end now. When Alistair sat next to her, leaning across to see what she was doing, she felt the warmth of his body tingling through hers.

'So…um…do you have some questions?'

'Yes. There are only a couple…' He leaned towards her, closing the lid of her laptop. Raina could hardly think straight. His scent was driving her crazy.

'What…?'

'Are you finding it as difficult to concentrate on this as I am?'

'Yes.' She leaned forward and kissed him. Just a brush against his cheek, which did nothing to slake the desire that was throbbing through her veins.

'Next question, then. How's your diary?' Alistair's fingers curved around hers, and he pressed them to his lips.

'Free. Completely.'

'Mine too.'

They wanted the same thing. But Alistair's

slow caress, the way he let each moment hang in the air, full of passion and expectation, was too good to miss. He kissed her, allowing nothing but their lips to touch, and the sensation was electrifying.

'I still want you, Raina. I can't help it.'

'That's all right. I can't help it either.' She slid closer to him, wrapping her arms around his neck, and when he kissed her again everything dissolved. Tomorrow could look after itself, all that mattered was that she had him in her arms now.

There was no rush. Alistair trailed kisses across her cheek, whispering the things she wanted to hear. By the time they got to their feet, they were moulded together, like two halves of a whole. He broke their embrace for one moment to reach for the partly finished bottle of wine and two glasses from the dresser.

'Come upstairs.'

'Yes...'

CHAPTER THIRTEEN

ALISTAIR HAD HELD her hand tight, rushing her up the stairs, the bottle and glasses held precariously in his other hand. When he kicked the bedroom door closed behind them, Raina pushed him back against it.

'Stay there.' She took the bottle and put it beside the bed, loosening the stopper and pouring half a glass of wine. She could feel Alistair's gaze on her. That was exactly what she wanted.

She walked back towards him, giving him the glass and kissing him lightly on the lips. Then she backed away. 'Don't move…'

He knew exactly what she was about to do. 'That's easier said than done, Raina.'

'Do your best.'

His best was always breath-taking, even if it was just watching. Raina slowly took her clothes off, and his gaze followed every movement. When she ran her hands over her body, he caught his breath and suddenly it felt as if Alistair was touching her.

'Raina…honey…' He groaned as she approached him, pressing her body against his. She took the glass from his hand, taking a mouthful and then giving it back to him. Alistair drained it, and let it fall to the floor.

She pulled his shirt over his head, running her hands across his chest. Raina could feel his heart beating. His hands caressed her back, barely touching her. She wanted more but she knew he wouldn't give it to her just yet. She popped open the button on the waistband of his jeans, feeling his body shiver against hers.

'Raina…' There was a note of desperation in his voice. 'One more move…'

'And what?' She teased him.

'You'll find out.'

Slowly she slid the zipper of his jeans down, her fingers caressing him. One sharp intake of breath and she suddenly found herself lifted off her feet and into his arms. She wound her legs around his waist as he strode across the room, bending to lay her down on the bed.

'You are in *so* much trouble…' His smile, as he knelt over her, kicking his shoes off and tugging at his jeans, told her that it was exactly the kind of trouble she wanted. The kind she'd dreamed about.

He made her happy. Raina and Alistair had gone over every detail of the prosthetics project together, anticipating problems and making plans for the next group of parents and children. They'd spent time with Anya, taking her out to places that they both loved in London, as if they were a real family. And they'd spent time alone, nights of lovemaking that brought them closer than they'd ever been, and that overwrote the pain.

Two weeks had seemed like a lifetime. It had changed the present, and maybe it could change their future. But, still, Raina knew that she had to be cautious. It wouldn't take much for it all to come crashing down.

Alistair was out of the office today, and he'd left her a package, wrapped in red tissue paper. When she opened it, it was a key ring, with a sparkly brick dangling from the chain. Even before she read the note, she knew what this was. She'd seen him put the first brick that Anya had picked up with her new hand into his pocket, and he'd made this so that she could carry it with her always.

She dialled his number, wondering if he'd answer, and the call went straight to voicemail. Some things didn't change. When Alistair was working, he devoted all his energies to the task.

'I love the key ring! Thank you. I'll see you later.' Raina left a message instead. However fragile this new relationship was, however fraught with danger, she couldn't wait to see Alistair tonight...

Alistair had been looking forward to seeing Raina all day. But when she opened her front door to him, something about the embarrassed way that she put her finger over her lips told him that rushing her inside and leaving their clothes scattered in the hallway and up the stairs wasn't going to be a good idea.

'What's up?'

Raina shut the door behind him and beckoned him into the kitchen.

'Anya's here.'

'Your mother couldn't take her tonight?' Anya's presence wasn't the disappointment that it might have been. If Raina let him stay, then the idea that they might both put the little girl to bed, and then retire downstairs to the sofa for just one kiss was…not quite as exciting perhaps, but it triggered a warmth in a deeper level of his soul.

She pressed her lips together, and sudden panic flowed through his veins. 'Is she all right?'

'Yes…yes, she's fine. I tried to call you…'

Guilt edged out the panic. Something was obviously up, and Raina had tried to call him. Alistair took his phone from his pocket, switching it on, and her missed calls and messages displayed on the screen.

'I'm sorry. I was in a meeting all day and…' He'd switched his phone off. Just as he'd done the day that Raina had lost their baby. Had he learned nothing?

Raina brushed his apology away. 'It's okay. Anya took a tumble and Mum was worried about her, so she took her down to the local hospital to get her checked out. By the time I'd got back from central London, she'd been seen and was ready to go. She's okay, but I wanted to bring her home tonight, just to keep an eye on her.'

'What happened?' Something cold clawed at Alistair's heart.

'She has a few bumps and bruises, and a cut on her forehead, which needed a couple of stitches. They made sure she didn't have a concussion...' Raina smiled. 'I did too when I got her home. I think I was still overreacting a bit.'

'It's not an overreaction. I'm tempted to check her over myself right now. You said she has stitches?'

'Yes, just here.' Raina brushed her forehead. 'The cut's right on her hairline, and the doctor who saw her did a very good job. It's not going to scar.'

And it had all happened while he'd been working. Anya had been hurt and Raina had rushed home. And Alistair had gone on with his day, pretty much as his father had done when his elder brother had broken his arm.

'May I see her?' Alistair didn't feel he had any right to ask.

'Yes, of course you can.' Raina stretched up, kissing his lips, but he hardly felt her touch. 'Don't look so worried. She's all right.'

That didn't make any difference. He wouldn't have known, whatever had happened. But

Raina's gaze was searching his face now, and she seemed anxious. Alistair reached for her, winding his arm around her waist and pulling her close.

'Yeah. Sorry, I just...' He searched for an excuse. 'She's had enough of hospitals to last her for the rest of her life.'

'Yes, I know. When Mum called I panicked a bit. I can't help it after what happened to Andrew and Theresa. But she's okay, so I think it's best we don't make too much fuss about it. If she wants to talk let her, but let's not put our own fears into her head.'

'No. That's very sensible.' Alistair leaned down, kissing her. Nothing. He felt nothing but the numbing effects of the guilt that weighed on his chest. And Raina's kiss was usually enough to make the heart of a statue beat faster.

'I'm sorry...about tonight.'

'What?' Suddenly the reason for Raina's hesitancy hit him. She was thinking that it was all just sex to him, and that he didn't want the complications of a child. 'Don't be crazy, Raina. I'm just worried about Anya. Would it be okay if I stayed awhile, maybe read her a story or something?'

Raina grinned suddenly. 'That would be great. Go on through, I'll be with you in a minute.'

Maybe it was by design, and maybe Raina really did have something to do in the kitchen, but Alistair was glad of the chance to be alone with Anya, to make sure for himself that she was all right. When he entered the sitting room, she was watching a cartoon on TV.

'Uncle Alistair!' Anya scrambled down from the sofa, and ran towards him for a hug. Alistair picked her up in his arms.

'How's my best girl?'

'I fell over. And Granny fell over. So we all went to the hospital.' Anya seemed keen to tell him her big news.

'Grandad took you?'

She nodded. 'And Granny had a big bandage on her. And the man put my head back together again.'

Alistair grinned. Anya was obviously milking this as much as she could. 'Right. Well, that's good, isn't it.'

Anya nodded. 'And he looked at my hand.'

'You hurt your hand as well?' Alistair picked up Anya's hand, inspecting it.

'No. My magic hand. He said it was fantastic. And that I'm a clever girl.'

'Well, he was quite right. You are.' Alistair looked up as Raina entered the room.

'She was quite the centre of attention. You showed the doctor how you curl your fingers up, didn't you, Anya.'

Anya nodded. 'He said that was fantastic too.'

'Yes, he did.' Raina kissed her daughter, and produced a storybook from behind her back. 'Would you like Alistair to read you a story before you go to bed?'

'Yes!'

When Alistair sat down on the sofa, Anya curled up in his lap, clearly wanting a little comfort despite her bravado. He opened the book, starting to read, and Raina sat down next to him, leaning against his shoulder. When he put his arm around her shoulders, it felt as if this was all he'd ever wanted but didn't deserve.

Alistair had carried Anya up to bed, and Raina had kissed her goodnight. When they reached the bottom of the stairs together, she suddenly seemed very weary.

'Why don't you go and sit down? I'll go and see what's cooking...' The smell coming from the kitchen had told Alistair that Raina had already put their dinner in the oven.

She smiled at him. 'Would you? Today's taken it out of me a bit.'

It would have been a difficult day for anyone. But seeing Anya at the hospital must have reawakened all the memories of Andrew and Theresa's accident. The grief, coupled with the need to look after their child, must have been overwhelming for her.

They ate, and Alistair insisted that Raina take a glass of wine into the sitting room while he cleared away the things. When he came to join her, she was asleep on the sofa. He sat for a while, listening to the silence, broken only by Raina's regular breathing.

He watched her sleep for a while and finally he woke her, ready to bid her goodnight and go, even though this was the only place he wanted to be tonight. But Raina sleepily asked that he stay, and he couldn't refuse her anything.

There was a first time for everything, and

sleeping with his hearing aid still in his ear wasn't as uncomfortable as he'd expected, as long as he lay on his right side. The sheets and pillows seemed to crackle whenever he moved, but at least he'd hear Anya if she woke. Alistair curled his body protectively around Raina's and she snuggled against him. As she drifted off to sleep, she murmured words that rent his heart.

'Thank you for being here, Alistair.'

'Where else am I going to be? Go to sleep now.'

He lay awake for a long time, staring into the darkness. This had to end. Not tonight, when Raina needed someone there to hold her, but soon. Despite all of her optimism, all her drive to make a better future for herself and Anya, Raina was still vulnerable. Still alone with a child, and still grieving the loss of her brother and his wife. She needed to go out and find someone who'd be her rock.

And Alistair knew her. Raina would always see her relationship with him, however uncommitted, as a reason not to look elsewhere. She would be faithful to him, even though he didn't have the right to expect it. Today hadn't been just an unfortunate oversight, he'd switched his phone off without a thought that Raina might need him. His work mattered and he would probably do the same again.

It hurt more than he could have imagined, but he had one more night. One night when he could watch over the two people who meant more to him than anyone. He wouldn't waste a moment of it in sleep.

Alistair had seemed tired the following morning. But he'd insisted on staying for breakfast, removing the dressing on Anya's forehead and examining the stitches carefully. It was only after he'd made sure that she was all right that he'd left, saying that he had some work to catch up on. Raina had thought about protesting that it was Saturday morning, and that she was sure that whatever it was could wait, but didn't. Their relationship was so new, and failure had made them both cautious. If, by some chance, they could find a way to succeed this time, it would be a result of taking things slow and steady.

They were both busy. Raina was putting the finishing touches to her talk and meeting with Gabriel to discuss the parent support programme. Alistair was working with the Dream Team on future improvements to the prosthetics, and the rest of his time was spent out of the office, visiting families who had applied to be part of the scheme. She didn't expect to be able to spend any time with Alistair until the weekend, and the thought that she might see him then was like a golden glow on the horizon, pulling her forward.

Alistair's text came unexpectedly on Wednesday evening, asking if he could drop round. Raina texted back a yes and put a bottle of wine in the fridge to cool. Alistair always made it sound as if his visits were going to be short, but they never turned out that way. But when she opened the door to him, his brow was creased.

'What's the matter?' She ushered him through to the kitchen. A cup of tea seemed like a better bet than wine. Clearly he had something he wanted to talk about.

As she made the tea and placed the cups on the table, he looked at her. 'I think—we should stop, Raina.'

Stop? Stop *what* exactly? It wasn't like Alistair to come straight out with something, he always thought about it first, and he'd obviously done his thinking without her.

'What…do you mean?' She sank down into a chair at the kitchen table, wrapping her hands around her teacup.

'I think that we should end our relationship. That doesn't make any difference to the work we've been doing at the charity. Gabriel will make sure that all of Anya's needs are met going forward, and I'll ask him to take over my work with you on the parent support programme…' He sat down slowly. 'But you and I can't be together any more.'

It made *all* the difference. To everything. Raina had dared to think that, in time, Alistair might be a husband again. A father this time.

Steady. Steady… She had to think about what he was saying, not just blurt out the first thing that came into her head. Raina took a breath, sipping her tea.

'Alistair, if this is about what happened last Friday, then…' She shrugged. 'Don't beat yourself up about it. Anya was all right, everyone was all right'

She'd made the same mistake all over again, and told him that it didn't matter whether he was there or not. Raina saw Alistair's face darken.

'You're saying it was easy to go to the hospital and fetch her?'

'No, it was harder than I'd thought it would be. I couldn't help thinking about her in that hospital bed after Andrew and Theresa died. She was so small, and she'd lost so much, her parents, her arm…' Tears started to run down Raina's cheeks. Alistair reached forward as if to brush them away, and Raina batted his hand to one side.

'Don't do that. Not when you're talking about leaving me.'

He nodded, as if he understood. Damn him, if he understood this anger, this pain, he wouldn't just walk away from her.

'What happened last Friday made me think about who I can and can't be. I just can't be what you both need.'

'Ah, and it's all your father's fault, is it?' He was going, and she may as well say it. 'It's not. It's *your* choice and you need to own it, Alistair. This is nothing to do with me, or what

I expect from you, and it's nothing to do with your father. It's about you.'

He stared at her and for a moment Raina wondered whether he'd been listening at all in the past few weeks. The blank-eyed look that invited her to throw whatever she wanted at him because he could take it was exactly the same one that had watched her leave the last time.

Well, this time he was going to have to do the leaving. Suddenly his face softened, and Raina wondered if he could go through with it. Then what would she do?

'Raina, I know. All I've ever achieved, everything I've done right is my work. I realise I have to reassess those priorities if I'm to be a part of your life, and I'm not sure that I can.'

'And you won't even try?' Raina knew now. This was the second time he'd done this to her, and she couldn't forgive him. Not even if he begged, and she was quite sure he wouldn't do that.

'I can't risk...' He was silent, shaking his head. Apparently she wasn't going to be privy to what Alistair could and couldn't risk.

'Go, then. Just go.' She would have shouted

the words if Anya hadn't been asleep upstairs. But lack of volume didn't change the way they sounded. Bitter and hurt. Which was just the way Raina felt.

He stared at her for a moment. Then he got to his feet, turning his back on her and walking out of the kitchen and into the hallway. Raina leaned forward, watching as he opened the front door. One last, treacherous impulse made her silently beg that he'd turn and look back.

But he didn't. The front door closed quietly behind him. If she knew Alistair at all, he definitely wasn't coming back.

She walked slowly to the door, laying her hand on the latch. The last thing he'd touched. Sadness and anger clawed in her heart, and she slammed her fist hard against the door, then sank to the floor behind it and started to cry.

A sound from upstairs stopped her short. She must have woken Anya. Raina wiped at her face with her sleeve, trying to rub away the tears. Taking a breath to steady herself, she walked upstairs to Anya's room.

'Mummy...?' The little girl was sitting up

in her bed, rubbing her eyes drowsily. Raina hugged her, laying her back down again.

'What's the matter, sweetie?'

'I heard a noise.'

'Ah. Well, everything's all right. Mummy just dropped something.' Dropped and smashed. Into so many pieces that it could never be put together again. 'Go back to sleep, darling.'

Anya nodded, closing her eyes, and then opened them again. 'Don't do it again, Mummy.'

Raina smiled, kissing her daughter. 'No, sweetie. I promise I won't do it again.'

CHAPTER FOURTEEN

'WHAT HAVE YOU DONE, Alistair?' Gabriel blustered into his office, slamming the door. 'It's been two weeks!'

'Take a seat, Gabriel.' Alistair waved his friend towards the armchairs at the other end of his office and Gabriel ignored him. Alistair's Italian wasn't up to much, but he knew when he was being cursed and called an idiot.

Heidi was outside, pulling her coat on to leave for the evening. She aimed a wave at the office, and then made herself scarce. These explosions happened from time to time, and they always blew over.

Gabriel was pacing, waiting for Heidi to go. When the outer office was empty, he walked over to the desk, planting his hands onto it. 'What did you do to her, Alistair?'

'Who?' He was too tired to feign ignorance and be convincing about it. He hadn't been sleeping and every waking moment had been consumed with thoughts of Raina. The happy times gave him as much pain as the bad times.

'You know who. First of all you ask me to help Raina with the induction course...'

'I explained all that to you, I'm trying to catch up on everything else. How's she doing?'

'Fine. Really well. You'd know that if you took the time to come over to the training suite.'

The training suite had been a life-saver. Alistair had been wondering how they were going to find the space to run induction courses, and DeMarco Pharmaceuticals had offered the training rooms in their London office. Raina had been spending all of her time there, and she obviously felt the same way as Alistair did. That they had nothing more to say to each other.

'As I said, I've been busy. And I do appreciate your stepping in.'

Gabriel rolled his eyes. 'You mean you appreciate me helping you to avoid Raina. She looks as if she hasn't had a wink of sleep, she doesn't come here and you don't go there. Normally I'd assume that you were engaging in an affair and being over-discreet about it, but she's miserable as well. I caught her crying the other day…'

Raina had been crying? Alistair wanted to rush to her, but that wasn't going to do any good. His presence in her life again would only make things worse.

'What…? Did you ask her why?'

'No, I just left her to it.' Gabriel's tone took on a note of sarcasm. 'Of *course* I asked her why. She said it was nothing. Which I took to mean that it was something. You…' Gabriel pointed accusingly at him.

Guilty as charged. 'If Raina didn't want to tell you, I'm certainly not going to.'

'Oh, for goodness' sake, Alistair…' Gabriel turned and started to pace again. 'I'm your friend.'

'Yes, and I appreciate the concern.' There was no doubt in Alistair's mind that this *was* concern. A little too much for him to deal with at the moment, but that was Gabriel's way.

'Look…maybe I can help. Not that I'm really the one to ask about relationship problems…'

'Clara might disagree.' Alistair switched the subject to the one person who was guaranteed to make Gabriel smile.

'Well, Clara's the one relationship I've managed to get right. I put that particular miracle down to her, not me.'

'You were the one who dropped everything and went to Mexico.'

Gabriel shrugged. 'I couldn't help that. Look, if Raina makes you happy…'

He *had* been happy. And being without her was tearing Alistair apart. 'We divorced, remember? It didn't work for us.'

'There's such a thing as a second chance, Alistair. You can't walk away and leave her hating you.'

Alistair shook his head. Gabriel didn't understand, Raina had told him she'd never hated him…

'Did she say that, Gabriel?' Hope began to tear at him as he realised just what his friend had said.

'What, that she hated you?' Gabriel shrugged. 'Does it matter? Clearly she does.'

'It matters. Did she say it?'

Gabriel pursed his lips. 'Well, I tried to get her to talk, and… Yes. She said it. More to shut me down than anything, I think.'

Alistair shot to his feet, rounding the desk

and enveloping his friend in a bear hug. 'There's something you can do for me.'

'What's that? Write a prescription?' Gabriel was looking at him as if he'd gone completely mad.

'No. A favour…'

Raina knew that the blonde woman who had entered DeMarco Pharmaceuticals' training suite had to be Clara. Not because she was obviously in the early stages of pregnancy, or because Gabriel greeted her with a kiss on the cheek. Gabriel had a habit of kissing anyone he hadn't seen for a while. It was because they seemed two parts of a whole somehow.

They were engrossed in conversation, not touching but the closeness was palpable. Then Clara smiled at her husband and turned, walking towards Raina.

'Hi, I'm Clara.' She held out her hand, her smile frank and open. Raina liked her already.

'I'm Raina. What do you think?' She swept her finger, pointing at the display boards that had been fixed to the walls.

'I think it's great. I was looking at them just now, and it's just the right mix of information, along with a little something to stir the imagination.' Clara grinned, pointing towards the image of Anya, using her prosthetic hand to play with her bricks. 'That's your daughter?'

'Yes. Anya…' The one little piece of light in the gloom. Raina had held onto her little girl, trying to subsume her sadness into a determination for a brighter future. That future was for Anya alone, though.

'She's beautiful.'

'I hear you're expecting twins. Congratulations.'

Clara grinned. It was nice to see someone so happy. 'Thank you. Gabriel just happened to mention it, did he?'

'Once or twice. He seems to be doing pretty well with the father-in-training routine.'

'Just wait until he finds out about changing nappies.' Clara chuckled. 'Gabriel says that it's Anya's birthday in ten days' time, and that you're planning a party.'

Planning a party wasn't quite the description. Gabriel had asked what Raina would be doing for Anya's birthday and she'd told him that she'd asked a few friends to the house.

'I haven't really decided what to do yet.'

'That's what I wanted to ask you about. We're having a party this weekend, and we've had a marquee put up in the garden. As it's there, we wondered if you'd like to use it for Anya's party.'

'That would be great but—you don't want half a dozen kids with their sticky fingers all over your house, do you?'

'I don't mind. And as you say, Gabriel's in training. He hardly flinches when I drop jam on the carpet these days.'

The image of red wine stains on the carpet hit Raina from nowhere. Alistair's bedroom and making love. He'd dropped his glass and they hadn't noticed the stain on the carpet until the following morning. Alistair had just smiled, telling her that they'd just made a memory.

One that hurt now. Raina took a breath. 'How big is the marquee?'

'It takes forty people. And there's room for a bouncy castle as well…' Clara was clearly making plans.

'There are a few extra people I could ask. Heidi and the Dream Team have been so good to Anya.'

'That's great. Ask them all.'

'I'll come and help decorate the marquee...'
Raina was beginning to get excited about the
prospect.

'Let me.' Clara leaned forward. 'I'm already
a bit fed up with this bee that Gabriel's got in
his bonnet about my resting all the time. It'll
be my pleasure.'

'Are you sure?'

'Positive. Give me your number and I'll call
you if I have any questions. I expect I'll have
plenty.'

'Thank you, Clara. This is really nice of you
and Gabriel.' Raina suspected that this was a
plan that they'd cooked up between them to
cheer her up. But Anya would love a party in
a marquee, and Raina was already beginning
to look forward to it.

'I'm so glad you've agreed.' Clara reached
into her bag, locating her mobile phone immediately. Raina would have to mention that when
she became a mother, her handbag might be
less organised. Another jab to the heart, as she
remembered the joke about the safety pins in
Alistair's mother's bag on their wedding day.

Leave it. Don't think about that, just look

to the future. Raina found her own phone, the screen smudged with sticky finger marks where Anya had been playing with it. She'd made a friend today, and if Gabriel and Clara were close to Alistair, then they seemed to both understand the situation and were tactfully working around it.

'You're really sure about this? When I give you my number it's a done deal.' Raina grinned.

'Quick, then. Give me the number.'

It was a bright, warm September day. Anya was running around, squealing with excitement, in the little pink princess costume that Raina had made for her, granting wishes with her sparkly wand. Raina's had already been granted. Seeing her little girl so happy was all she wanted.

She'd offered to go and help with the preparations for the party this morning, and Clara had given an obstinate no. An hour early would be more than enough. When she parked outside the house, the swathe of pink and mauve balloons around the front door showed her that she was in the right place. Gabriel flung the door open before she and Anya had even got out of the car, and Anya ran up the front steps.

'Happy birthday, Anya!' He scooped her up in his arms and Anya tapped him on the top of his head with her wand.

'Wish granted!'

Gabriel chuckled. 'Thank you. Let's see if we can find a few wishes for you, shall we?'

Outside, a bouncy castle sat next to a large marquee, one side of which was covered with a hoarding that had been painted to look just like a castle, with turrets and people along the battlements. Gabriel showed Anya where to tap her wand, and the door swung open.

The inside of the marquee continued the castle theme. A long banqueting table stood at one end, low enough for the children to sit at. Around the edge of the marquee was a frieze with medieval lords and ladies painted on it, and on one side there were doors to open and tunnels to run through. There was a dragon, with a wide grin on its face, holding a cauldron in one hand and a red sparkly button in the other, and Clara walked up to it, bending down to press the button. The lid of the cauldron swung open and Clara could see small gold-wrapped packages inside.

'Gabriel! This is gorgeous. How long did Clara spend doing all of this?'

Gabriel dismissed the question. 'Hardly any time at all. You like it, Anya?'

Anya nodded, running to explore the rest of the tent. Every part of it contained something different and imaginative to catch a child's attention. Clara must have had professional help with this.

'That'll be a yes.' Raina turned to Gabriel. 'She loves it and she'd like to thank you and Clara very much.'

Gabriel chuckled. 'No thanks needed. As long as she enjoys herself...' He turned, as the sound of the doorbell echoed faintly through from the open back door. 'That'll be the unicorn.'

'The what?'

'Actually, it's a Shetland pony. But it has a horn on its bridle and Clara reliably informs me that it's impossible to tell the difference. I'll have to get them to walk it down the road and bring it through the alleyway at the back as it might take fright and stampede if we bring it through the house. Where's Anya got to?'

'Hiding in the magic forest.' In one corner of the marquee there was a selection of small artificial trees, with twinkly lights in them. 'Anya…'

Anya appeared from behind a tree, running back to Raina and trying to pull her back to the forest for a game of hide and seek. Gabriel bent down to her, tapping her on the shoulder.

'Would you like to come and see the unicorn with me? Mummy can stay here and guard the castle.'

Anya looked at Raina and she nodded. 'That sounds fun. Where's Clara, Gabriel? I have to go and thank her, this is so beautiful.'

'Um…lying down. Give her fifteen minutes. I'll bring you a glass of wine to fortify you for the fray…' He shot the words over his shoulder as Anya tugged at his sleeve, propelling him out of the tent.

A moment later he was back, a chilled glass of white wine in one hand and Anya's hand held firmly in the other.

'Mummy, there's a unicorn! I saw it out the window!'

'Did you, darling?' Raina smiled at her. 'Go with Gabriel, then, and you might be able to say hello to it.'

'What's its name?'

'I don't know. You'd better ask Gabriel.' Raina shot him a smile.

'Um… I don't know either. You have to ask it. I believe that it's only allowed to tell you if you're four years old.'

'I'm four!' Anya was dancing on the spot, pulling at Gabriel's hand as he led her back out of the tent.

It was all so beautiful. Twinkling lights, games for the children. There were even little tubs of glitter jelly on the table. Raina sipped her wine, feeling a tear prick at the side of her eye. The one thing that would make it all beyond perfect was sharing it with… She turned as she heard the door to the tent swing open behind her.

Alistair! Raina blinked, wondering if this really was a magic castle and just thinking about him had conjured him up. But he seemed real enough, walking towards her with that awkward smile on his face that she loved so very much.

Now wasn't the time to run into his arms. It wasn't the time to punch him for having hurt her so much either. Raina stared at him only half-aware that the glass had slipped from her hand and fallen onto the grass.

'Does Anya like the tent?'

Something about the way he looked around gave Raina an inkling that he might have had a hand in all this. 'Did *you* do this, Alistair?'

'Um…yes. I did.' Suddenly he puffed out a breath. 'I wanted to do something for Anya so I took the liberty of asking Gabriel for his help…'

She'd get to Gabriel later. He and Clara had clearly been in on a subterfuge and she'd let them know that she knew. But remembering the delight on Anya's face when she'd seen the tent, she couldn't find it in her heart to blame them for it.

But she had questions. Important ones.

'You did *all* of it?'

'Not quite. Clara iced the cake, because I made a complete mess of it.' He pointed to the cake, which had pink sparkly frosting and an icing-sugar castle on it. 'She came with me to check the unicorn out as well.'

'Wait… Alistair, are you telling me you made a cake?' *That* would be a first. 'I thought you were at a conference in Scotland this week.'

He shifted uncomfortably from one foot to the other. 'We sent someone else, and I took the week off. And, yes, unlikely as it might seem, I made a cake.'

It was make or break time. Raina could either send him away now or she could ask.

Asking probably wouldn't do any good. It would only break her heart again. But if there was a one in a million chance, Raina knew that she had no option but to take it. Before she had a chance to think about it any more, she found herself walking towards him.

'Why did you do all this, Alistair?'

'You told me that I could be whoever I wanted to be. That it was my choice, and I had to own it.' He grinned suddenly. 'This is who I want to be.'

Raina felt herself begin to tremble. 'Couldn't you just have said so?'

He shook his head. 'No, I don't think that would have been enough. I had to prove that I could do it. To myself and then to you.'

A lump formed in her throat. Raina was

so used to thinking of Alistair as everything she wanted and couldn't have. But if he could change, then she could too.

'It's beautiful, Alistair. And doing it all your-self...' Tears formed in her eyes. 'No one could have done any better than this. If you ever had to prove yourself to me, you've done it.'

He *had* proved himself. A week of hard work wasn't all that unusual, but getting to grips with what would delight a four-year-old had been more puzzling. Clara had finally brushed away his questions, reminding him that he'd been a child once, and telling him to just get in contact with that much-neglected part of his psyche.

It had hurt, a lot more than he'd expected. Making the cake had been simpler than he'd thought, just a matter of buying the ingredients and following the recipe carefully. But he'd sat in the kitchen, inspecting its progress through the glass door of the oven, and tears had rolled down his face. His father would never have considered that the cost of time, instead of money, was a reasonable bargain.

'It's been an interesting week. And, yes, I did

prove it to myself.' He'd left a part of himself behind as well. The part that was bound by his own childhood. And as he'd turned away from that, he'd seen a future that was lit by all the possibilities he'd thought were lost to him.

'Thank you, Alistair. It's perfect.'

'There's something else, Raina.'

'Yes, I've heard all about the unicorn...'

'No, not the unicorn. I love you and I know you love me.'

She flushed suddenly, staring at him. For a moment Alistair wondered if he'd been wrong and had built a castle out of sand, but something in her eyes told him that he was right.

'Raina, you told Gabriel that you hated me. I know you, you don't hate anyone. You'd only say that if someone you loved hurt you. And I know that I did hurt you, very badly.'

'Yes...you did.'

'I'm sorry for that, Raina. And I know I'll have to work to win you back, but I love you. I've always loved you, and that's never going to change.'

Tears welled in her eyes, and Alistair saw all the pain. And all the love. Suddenly Raina threw her arms around his neck.

'Alistair, I love you too. I'll always want you, through the good times and the bad…'

'You…do?' Loving him was all he'd dared hope for. He'd thought that it would take time before Raina could allow herself to rely on him again.

'Yes, I do. We can deal with whatever life throws at us together.'

He was helpless now. Bound by magic, silken ropes that were worthy of any self-respecting magic castle. Alistair kissed her cheek, gently disentangling himself from her embrace. There was one more thing that he had to do.

Falling to one knee, he reached for her hands, holding them in his.

'Marry me, Raina. This is the second time I've asked and this time it's for keeps. I won't let anything break us apart.'

Raina felt a tear roll down her cheek. This sudden realisation of all the dreams she'd tried to deny had brought her to a stumbling point. 'I want to say yes more than anything, Alistair. But it would be selfish of me. You want a family, and I might not be able to give you—'

He reached up, laying his finger against her

lips. 'You and Anya are the only family I need. We'll have enough love to meet anything that the future holds.'

'But—'

'Trust me, Raina.'

She did trust him. And she loved him. Raina fell to her knees, kissing him.

'Yes, Alistair. Yes...'

She felt his chest heave, as if he'd been holding his breath. Then he took hold of her hand. 'I have a ring.' He said the words almost shyly.

'A ring? You mean you had this all planned?'

'I planned the party. Everything else was a hope that I was determined to make into a reality one day.' He raised her hand to his lips, kissing her finger and then slipping the ring onto it. Three stones flashed brightly in the sunlight.

'The two diamonds on either side are from your old engagement ring.'

Raina felt her breath catch. 'You kept it?'

'I never stopped loving you, Raina. Even when I didn't know it. This one is new...' He brushed his thumb against larger stone in the centre. 'That's for the future. Because I never *will* stop loving you.'

'It's lovely, Alistair. And I love the thought behind it even more.' She felt tears in her eyes again, and when he brushed them away with his finger, she knew that this was how it was going to be from now on. Alistair would be there for her, always. He got to his feet, lifting her with him, and then wound his arms around her.

She could hear the sound of Anya's excited chatter outside, and reckoned that the unicorn had made it round to the garden. But she still had time to kiss Alistair again.

'Our own magic castle. I love you so much, Alistair.'

The afternoon passed in a daze of happiness. Raina had shown Clara her ring, and she'd screamed and flung her arms around her. The guests started to arrive and Gabriel turned his attention to organising the unicorn rides. Alistair had momentarily left Raina's side to watch as Anya opened her presents.

Raina could see the tension on his face as Anya opened the package that he'd brought for her, but Anya knew what it was straight away. The pink, sparkly princess arm that she'd said she wanted. Alistair was all smiles as he helped Anya take off the flesh-coloured prosthetic and put the new one on.

'Can you do that?' Sam Ross had been unable to take up a place in the pilot project because he was recovering from an operation, but he was a regular visitor at The Watchlight Trust's offices, and due to take a place with the next group. When he'd seen Anya's new arm, he'd dragged his mother over to where Raina was standing.

'Yes, we can do it.' Raina bent down to the child. 'Sam, what are you thinking? Would you like a superhero arm?'

'Yes, please.' Sam's reluctance to accept a prosthetic seemed to have been quashed.

'A superhero arm…?' Alistair had joined her again, his eyes still following Anya as she showed everyone her new arm, flexing the fingers to show them how it worked. 'That's a great idea.'

'Are you sure?' Sam's mother enquired.

'Ben's going to love that particular challenge.' Alistair smiled, putting his arm around Raina's shoulder. 'The design and the microelectronics are the same, it's just a different outer shell. Something the other kids can't do, eh, Sam? Be a superhero…'

Another little piece of love that had been spread this afternoon. If they weren't careful the tent was going to explode from the pressure of all the moments of magic that it contained.

At six o'clock the goodie bags were distributed, and the tent began to empty out. Clara and Gabriel found something in the house to catch Anya's attention, and Alistair and Raina were finally alone again.

'Clara and Gabriel have ordered us out of their garden.' Alistair folded her in his arms and kissed her. 'Clara says I can come back tomorrow to help clear up. But not until the afternoon.'

'Mmm. That's nice of them. What shall we do with ourselves until tomorrow afternoon?'

Alistair smiled. 'I'd like to go home, and spend the evening with my family.'

'That sounds nice. What then?'

He chuckled. 'I want to spend the first night of the rest of my life with my beautiful fiancée. Soon to be wife…'

He wanted all the same things that she did. And together they could make them a reality.

'That sounds perfect, Alistair.'

EPILOGUE

Exactly two years later

ALISTAIR HELPED HER out of the car, and Raina walked up the front path. Alistair followed, the same dopey grin on his face that he'd worn for the last thirty-six hours. He'd carried Raina over the threshold eighteen months ago after their wedding, and now he was about to do with same with their newborn son.

They'd explored all their options. It had taken a little medical intervention before Raina had been able to fall pregnant, but Alistair had taken much of the stress out of the process by telling her every day that he loved her and that he already had everything he wanted.

She put the key into the lock, twisting it and then pushing the front door open. Alistair took hold of her hand, and they stepped into the hallway together.

'Welcome home, Alexander James Duvall.'

Alistair took Alex from the baby carrier carefully, smiling down at him.

'Where is everyone?' Raina looked around. The house was suspiciously quiet.

'Come and sit down.' Clara appeared from the kitchen, taking Raina by the arm and leading her into the sitting room. 'Gabriel took the kids out into the garden. Anya was determined not to open any of her birthday presents until you were here…'

'Wow! It looks so nice in here. Are you sure that's enough balloons?' Two huge bundles of balloons were clustered on each side of the bay window, reaching from the floor to the ceiling.

'We reckoned that the pink ones would be for Anya and the blue for Alex.' Clara looked round as a muffled bang sounded from the garden. 'And the twins have found out that if you sit on a balloon it pops.'

Raina chuckled. Clara and Gabriel's eighteen-month-old twins were into all kinds of mischief, often egged on by their father. 'And who showed them how to do that?'

'Well, Anya's far too grown up for that kind of thing…' Clara chuckled. 'I'll go and tell them you're back.'

Alistair waited until Raina had made herself comfortable on the sofa and then delivered their sleeping boy into her arms. Sitting down next to her, he curled his own arms around them both.

'This is…' His expression was that of a man at the mercy of joy.

'Fleeting, I imagine.' Raina grinned at him.

'One moment is all I need.' He put his arms around her and kissed her.

They were interrupted as Anya tumbled into the room, followed by Gabriel, who had a twin under each arm. He sat them down on the floor and they both clambered to their feet, walking unsteadily towards the balloons. They'd clearly learned that a pincer movement meant that their father couldn't grab both of them at the same time, and as Gabriel picked Sofia up Pietro managed to reach the balloons, tugging at them.

'It's your own fault, Gabriel.' Clara entered with the cake. 'They weren't interested in the balloons until you started popping them.'

Gabriel chuckled. 'If they weren't so much like their mother, I'd find it easier to keep up with them.' He reached Pietro before he managed to pull the column of balloons down, swinging him up above his head, and the little dark-haired boy whooped with laughter.

Alex was still blissfully asleep in Raina's arms. Maybe he was dreaming of the warmth and the love that surrounded him. Alistair went to the kitchen, returning with a bottle of champagne and one of sparkling apple juice.

'Daddy iced my cake all by himself.' Anya wriggled up onto the sofa, and Raina put her arm around her daughter. It was a tradition now that Alistair make Anya's birthday cakes, and his icing skills were improving. This one had a dinosaur theme, with small models of dinosaurs ranging over an iced prehistoric landscape.

'I'm particularly proud of the triceratops.' Alistair twisted the cork in the champagne bottle, and the pop attracted the twins' attention. 'Presents first, or cake, Anya?'

'Presents!' Anya slid down from her seat, running to the fireplace and carefully sorting through the wrapped packages, deciding which to open first.

'Right, then. Presents and champagne.' Alistair passed the bottle to Gabriel, who started to fill the glasses that were laid out on the table next to the cake and reached for the bottle of apple juice. 'Special champagne for you, Anya, as it's your birthday. Raina?'

'I'll have a few sips of the real stuff.' It would probably go straight to her head, but nothing could be as intoxicating as this.

'Right.' Alistair put a glass in her hand and raised his. 'A toast...'

They'd toasted the baby then Anya and then each other. Anya had opened her presents and they'd eaten cake. It had been a perfect afternoon.

Clara had taken little Alex, cooing over him and wondering aloud whether Gabriel missed that gorgeous baby smell as much as she did. Raina had seen the smile that flashed between them, and reckoned it wouldn't be very long before Clara was pregnant again. Alistair had suggested that Raina might like to lie down, and she suddenly felt very tired.

When she came back downstairs, the house was quiet. She could hear Alistair reading a story in the sitting room, and when she walked quietly through, she saw him. Anya was on his lap, and he held Alex carefully in front of her so she could put her arms around her new baby brother.

The book was propped open in front of them, and it didn't matter that he couldn't turn the pages. He'd read this story to Anya so often that he knew the words, and if he went wrong Anya was just as familiar with it and would correct him. The sound of his voice seemed already to have lulled Alex to sleep.

Raina crept into the room, sitting down quietly. He smiled up at her, and she nodded him on with the story. This moment was far too precious to interrupt.

Finally Anya's head started to droop against his chest. A moment later she was fast asleep, worn out by the excitement of the day. Alistair smiled, gesturing for Raina to take Alex while he carried Anya up to her bed. By the time he returned, Alex was settled into his Moses basket.

'So…' Alistair looked around the room. 'They're both asleep. What do we do now?'

'First you need to come over here. Then you can kiss me.'

'Ah, yes. Of course, I knew there was something, I'd forgotten.'

'Don't you dare ever forget that.' She felt his arms around her, and snuggled against him, knowing that whatever happened Alistair would always be there for her.

His chest heaved as a sigh of contentment escaped his lips. 'You know, I could really get used to this. I'm looking forward to the next six weeks. Just the four of us…'

'There might be times when you wish you could just put on a suit and go into the office. For a bit of peace and quiet…' Today had been a great day, but Raina was under no illusion that every day was going to be like this.

He raised one eyebrow. 'And who's going to rub your feet for you if I do that?'

'Good point. I hadn't taken that into consideration. And since you mention it…' Alistair did the very best foot massage and it was a little piece of intimacy that was very welcome right now.

He chuckled, shifting along the sofa and taking her feet on his lap. As he started to massage them, Raina relaxed.

'So what were you and Gabriel muttering about in the corner?'

'Work. It's the last time I'm going to say that word for another six weeks.'

'Oh. And since when did we not talk about work?'

'You've just had a baby. You don't need to bother about anything else other than recovering from that right now.'

'So I don't get an update on our new project?'

Now that the prosthetics project was a success, The Watchlight Trust had taken on a couple of new staff to help run it, and it wasn't taking up so much of their time. Alistair and Raina had made a shortlist of three new projects that they both felt passionate about, and had asked the Dream Team for their ideas on each of them.

Alistair narrowed his eyes. 'I told you. This time's for you.'

'Come here.' Raina crooked her finger and he leaned towards her. 'I love being your wife, and I love being a mother. I love being a doctor too, and not one of those things takes anything away from the others. You know how excited I am about starting a new project.'

He puffed out a breath. 'Okay. I get it. You want to see the detailed proposals that the Dream Team have come up with, don't you?'

'Now you've told me about them, I do. After I've had some more sleep, that is.'

'All right, here's the bargain. You submit to every last bit of pampering that I can muster, and I'll get them sent over. You can read through them if and when you feel ready.'

'Thank you, Alistair. I love you. And I love it that we can share every part of our lives with each other, at work and at home.'

He caught her hand in his, kissing her fingers. Then he repeated the promise he'd made to her on their wedding day. 'Always, Raina. Everything, always.'

* * * * *

LET'S TALK
Romance

For exclusive extracts, competitions and special offers, find us online:

- facebook.com/millsandboon
- @millsandboonuk
- @millsandboon

Or get in touch on 0844 844 1351*

For all the latest titles coming soon, visit millsandboon.co.uk/nextmonth

*Calls cost 7p per minute plus your phone company's price per minute access charge

Want even more
ROMANCE?

Join our bookclub today!

'Mills & Boon books, the perfect way to escape for an hour or so.'

Miss W. Dyer

'Excellent service, promptly delivered and very good subscription choices.'

Miss A. Pearson

'You get fantastic special offers and the chance to get books before they hit the shops'

Mrs V. Hall

Visit millsandbook.co.uk/Bookclub and save on brand new books.

MILLS & BOON